An unfamiliar thrill sent shivers of delight down her spine. She suddenly felt awkward, with her arms around his neck.

She glanced up shyly and dropped her arms, but still Montaigne held her loosely around the waist, as if he didn t want to let her go. His dark eyes gazed at her in a strangely intimate, questioning way. The way a man looked at a woman he found attractive . . . The heat began in Cicely s chest and rose to her head, until she felt uncomfortably hot and breathless. . . .

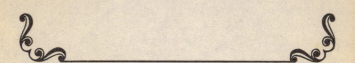

By Joan Smith
Published by Fawcett Books:

Books published by The Ballantine Publishing Group are available at quantity discounts on bulk purchases for premium, educational, fund-raising, and special sales use. For details, please call 1-800-733-3000.

A CHRISTMAS GAMBOL

Joan Smith

FAWCETT CREST • NEW YORK

A Fawcett Crest Book
Published by Ballantine Books
Copyright © 1996 by Joan Smith

All rights reserved under International and Pan-American Copyright Conventions. Published in the United States by Ballantine Books, a division of Random House, Inc., New York, and simultaneously in Canada by Random House of Canada Limited, Toronto.

http://www.randomhouse.com

Library of Congress Catalog Card Number: 96-96445

ISBN 0-449-22493-7

Manufactured in the United States of America

First Edition: November 1996

10 9 8 7 6 5 4 3 2 1

had penned *Chaos*, Cicely had not felt it necessary to remind her readers of the eye color in every chapter. She toyed with the notion of making more use of nature, throwing in a howling wind or a slashing rain to presage imminent danger. Yet a howling wind did not seem appropriate when the danger was so mundane as burning the marmalade, or a pig getting loose in the vegetable garden. Such were Georgiana's trials, for she was drawn from life, not the realm of fantasy.

Cicely's inspiration was not the anonymous lady who had penned *Chaos Is Come Again*, but the equally anonymous lady who had written *Pride and Prejudice*. Egerton had published the latter, which was why Cicely had sent *Georgiana* to him. Perhaps the anonymous author had worked "on commission." If only Cicely had two hundred pounds to risk, for it certainly was a risky venture. Mr. Egerton had made no bones about that. He wrote of hoping to recoup the investment, not making a profit.

Cicely's annual income was two hundred and fifty pounds, the interest on her dowry of five thousand. At her present rate of saving, it would take her five years to save two hundred pounds. Even a provincial lady, with plain hazel eyes in lieu of violet, and with chestnut hair instead of sable required an occasional new gown or bonnet.

Papa would never allow her to eat into her capital. Indeed she would not care to do it. Five thousand was little enough enticement to the gentlemen as it was. Her friend, Meg St. Clair, a beautiful, noble lady, had had to go to London to nab a *parti*. An untitled lady like herself, with no particular claim to beauty, needed all the dowry she could scrape together to secure a good match.

Elmdale, her papa's estate in Kent, was isolated from town. Papa had no use for company. He was happy with his books, his church work, and his work of raising hops. Anne, his elder daughter, had become his housekeeper when Mrs. Caldwell had died a decade earlier. To Cicely, only ten years old at the time, her mama was but a memory. On their weekly trip to the village, Cicely and Anne always stopped at the circulating library. Reading helped to pass the long evenings. When Cicely had read most of the novels there, she began writing one of her own. It had been a great solace during the quiet winter. In spring she had made a fair copy in her best copperplate hand; in the dead of summer she had begun sending it off to publishers. Now it was back, it was late November, and she was impatient for her work to reach the public.

She gazed out the library window to the park, where an autumnal wind tossed the stark branches of stately elms, sending down an occasional withered leaf. Soon there would be snow, and Christmas, then spring again. The uninterrupted rhythm of her life caused her a moment's ennui, until she remembered that she had those revisions to make to *Georgiana*. She strode purposefully to the table and sharpened her quill.

In London, Lord Montaigne pounced up the steps of a handsome mansion on Berkeley Square, gave one tap of the knocker, and entered his sister's house before the butler reached the door.

"It's only me, Coddle," he said. "Is Lady Fairly home?"

"In the saloon, milord. She is alone. I shall—"

"Don't bother. I'll announce myself," Montaigne

said. He stripped off his York tan gloves, his great-coat and curled beaver, and handed the lot to Coddle before sauntering toward the saloon.

From the vaulted archway, he saw his sister sliding a marble-covered novel under a pillow and smiled. Meg was seldom without a gothic novel at hand, on those rare occasions when she was alone. It was more usual to find her saloon littered with fashionable fribbles. Lady Margaret St. Clair had caused quite a stir when she had made her curtsey at St. James's two years before. Her Titian curls and sparkling brown eyes had set many a noble heart aflutter. In the twinkling of a bedpost she had landed an earl, married him, and set up as one of Society's leading hostesses.

"No, don't put it away," Montaigne said, sauntering forward. "It happens I want to talk to you about books."

"Oh, Monty. It's you." She smiled, holding out her dainty white hand. "I simply adored *Chaos Is Come Again.* I cannot believe you really wrote it. It is so unlike you." She patted the sofa beside her, urging him to sit down.

Montaigne lowered his tall, elegant body onto the striped sofa, crossed one leg over the other, and sighed. "For my sins," he said. "You have not told anyone my dark secret? It would quite knock the feathers off my dignity."

"Of course not, ninnyhammer. While it is an excellent novel of its sort, I am clever enough to realize it would not do for the Marquess of Montaigne to have penned it. Your budding career in Parliament would be over in a day. However did you come to do such a thing? I daresay it was Debora's marriage to the duke that set you off?"

"That, and my busted ankle," he said, his hand going instinctively to rub it, as it still caused pain if he was on his feet for long, and he had been speaking in the House for close to an hour that afternoon.

"I daresay it was the laudanum that set you off," Lady Fairly said. "There is a rumor running around town that Coleridge is writing a new poem that was incited by laudanum, but he woke up before it was finished. He has been trying forever to finish it, but cannot, so he is going to publish a part of a poem. Is that not droll? Something about Genghis Khan."

"Kubla Khan, actually," Montaigne amended. "Unlike Coleridge, my story came to me complete, only replacing the sybaritic luxuries of Xanadu with hell. Scribbling it down helped to pass the month I was laid up at the abbey after I took that tumble from Caesar. Being a cruel beast, I rather enjoyed watching Debora struggle through the mire of trials and tribulations I loaded on the poor girl. The writing had a therapeutic effect. It cured me of my boyish crush."

"I quite understand," Lady Fairly said. "When I am angry with Fairly, I imagine him losing all his money and having to beg in the street for a crust of bread. But then I realize that if he lost his blunt, he could not buy me such lovely gowns and jewels and things."

"That, of course, is a husband's prime function," Montaigne said blandly.

"Of course. So I let him recoup his fortune at the gaming table. What I cannot understand is why Debora chose the duke over you, for it is understating the matter to say he is plain, while you are shockingly handsome. If Morland's eyes bulged any farther they would leave his head entirely."

She smiled at her elder brother, whom she mentally conceded was almost as handsome as Fairly, and of course a good deal sharper. Monty was cut in the mold of a Corsair, tall and broad-shouldered, with black hair and a wicked dark eye. Were it not for his lips, which were more inclined to lift in laughter than to curl in a cynical sneer, he might be a pattern card for Byron's Corsair.

"I console myself that she chose a duke over a marquess—or her mama did," he replied.

As Lady Fairly poured two glasses of sherry and handed her brother one, she concluded that he had indeed recovered from his brief infatuation. No aura of heartbreak lingered on his healthy visage. No shadow marred his sparkling eyes.

"It is called a love match, actually—or was. The flames are fast dying to embers," Lady Fairly remarked. When Montaigne expressed no interest in this, she said, "What is it you want to discuss? You mentioned books. You know I would never reveal your secret about the book, dear Monty. I think it noble of you to give all the money to charity, when you could have bought dozens of horses or jackets or diamond necklaces for your sister. Even Fairly does not know who wrote *Chaos*, and I tell him everything—except how much money I owe and who my new flirts are. He is shockingly jealous." She smiled.

"My visit has to do with *Chaos*," he said, studying his sister and wondering if she would do. Dearly as he loved Meg, he realized her shortcomings. "The thing is, John Murray insists on meeting the authoress. When I submitted the novel to him, I implied the anonymous lady was a cousin. I acted as her agent and handled the contract and monies.

Now that it is a hit, he wishes to discuss her next book with her and to introduce her to the ton."

Lady Fairly gazed at Montaigne. "You want me to arrange for a wig and gown and so on? You will make a shockingly big lady, but I daresay if Murray spots the resemblance to yourself, he will think it is because you are your cousin."

"It was not a masquerade that I had in mind," he said firmly.

"Oh." She looked a question at him.

"No, what I was wondering was if you would mind saying you had written the thing."

"Me!" She clapped her hands in joy. "I should adore to! What a lark! But Murray knows I am not your cousin, Monty. He would think it excessively odd that I had ever made a secret of it in the first place, if I had written it." Her expression clouded to doubt. "Besides, everyone knows I can scarcely write an invitation without Fairly helping me. English is so horrid—all those letters that don't seem to make any sound when spoken. And when could I have had time to write it? I am trotting day and night."

Montaigne reluctantly accepted that no one would believe Meg capable of stringing two literate sentences together. "Can you suggest some discreet lady who would not object to pretending she had written the book?"

"Oh, Lord, Monty, none of my friends could keep a secret like that. They would be crowing from the rooftops." She sipped on her sherry for a moment, then continued. "What you should do is bring in some lady from the provinces. Let Murray meet her. Then pay her off and hustle her back out of town."

Monty listened with interest. Meg was as flighty

as a bird, but she was not entirely witless. "That is not a bad notion," he said. "Now, who? Cousin Edith, perhaps . . ."

"Foolish boy. Once you let *her* get her two feet in your house, you would have a pensioner for life. And the same of Cousin Elinor."

"I had thought of hiring an actress, but then she might be recognized."

"Or might hold you to ransom, threatening to tell the truth if you did not pay her shockingly large sums of money. To say nothing of the accent. They never get it quite right. No, what we want is some mousy creature from the country, someone we can trust implicitly. . . . But of course! Sissie Caldwell! She is my oldest and dearest friend—although I have not seen her since making my wedding. But we promised to keep in touch with letters."

"And did you?" he asked, pondering her suggestion.

"Well, I write her little notes occasionally, and she answers with nice, long letters full of news. Old Mr. Harper, who lived at Lily Bay and grew all those lovely lilies, died last month. His nephew inherited the place, but Sissie says he is an old, confirmed bachelor, which is a pity, for of course she hoped he would be young and handsome and marry her. Perhaps he would do for Anne."

Monty stirred restively.

"I have been meaning to write again," she continued. "In any case, she will love to do it for me. Sissie, you must know, is the very soul of discretion. And there is another bonus in using her. She will be familiar with *Chaos*, for she lives with her nose in a book. It was Sissie who introduced me to novels, back at the abbey. If Murray wants to discuss plots and characters and all those horrid technical things, she will know exactly what he is talking about, for Sissie spoke of writing a novel herself, when she wrote to me."

"She's rather young," Montaigne said uncertainly.

"Young? Why, she is my age—twenty years, and not a sign of a beau, poor girl."

"Twenty, eh? I had thought she was younger. Yes, Sissie would do very well. There is just one little detail. I cannot invite a young lady to stay with me."

"She will stay with me, of course. We are best friends, though I am not sure she'll approve of my new friends. It will not be a long visit, eh? And you will take her off my hands for most of the time. You mentioned Murray's wanting to meet her."

"Yes, he plans a dinner party in her honor."

"Will Byron be there?" Lady Fairly asked eagerly.

"No, of course not. He has retired to the country, and besides, one hears shocking stories about him. Shall I send Sissie an invitation?"

"It will be better if I call on her at Elmdale and explain the situation. I'll drive down tomorrow. Do you think she will agree to do it?"

"How can she refuse, when the money is to go to charity? Her papa is very churchy, you recall. You gave his cousin the living of St. Albans at home. He owes you a favor. Will you tell her who the real author is?"

"Good God, no!"

"You must give some excuse why the real author cannot come forward."

"A mere detail. I shall say she is ill, or too old to make the trip."

"Say it is our Aunt Ethel who wrote it."

"We don't number an Aunt Ethel among our dozen or so aunts—do we?"

"Of course not, goose. It is best to keep our real aunts out of it. Then it is all settled. You will leave for Elmdale tomorrow. Tell Sissie I'm looking forward to seeing her. I shall try to find her a *parti* while she is here, for there are no interesting gentlemen at home. Pity about Harper's nephew."

Monty felt a spasm of alarm. "Sissie is only staying a few days! It is crucial that she leave London very soon after meeting Murray."

"Two or three days may be long enough. You have heard of love at first sight, I suppose?"

"I have heard of it. I have also heard of the bogeyman and leprechauns and faithful women, but I take leave to doubt these chimera exist."

Lady Fairly shook her curls. "Spoken like a cynic. It is very difficult to believe you wrote such a shockingly romantic novel as *Chaos Is Come Again*. Will you do another book? You mentioned Murray suggested it."

"Perhaps, if I happen to break another ankle, simultaneously fall in love and get jilted, and the Tories stay in power. We can count on the last item at least. My work in the House is limited while they hold the reins. The orphanage could well use the blunt."

Montaigne rose and took his leave, for he feared Lord Fairly would be returning soon for dinner, and he always avoided that handsome mannequin when he could.

Chapter Two

Lord Montaigne arrived at Elmdale the next afternoon to find Miss Cicely and Miss Caldwell in their comfortable saloon, sewing cravats for their papa. The cozy fire crackling in the grate was welcome to ward off November's chilly blast. Although the sisters were surprised to receive a visit from Montaigne, they did not scramble to hide the linen and sewing box behind the sofa. Mr. Caldwell was well to grass, but he had not reared his daughters to indolence or frivolity or any worldly dissipation. Miss Caldwell had donned a cap the year before, to tell the world she no longer considered herself eligible for matrimony. As Montaigne was more interested in Miss Cicely, he took particular notice of her appearance. The word *provincial* was indelibly stamped on her unfashionable body.

She was modestly attired in a green and black striped flannel gown that did its best to conceal a rather buxom figure. Her chestnut curls were bound in a bun, from which a few wayward curls escaped to bounce over her ears. She might have been a vicar's daughter—or an anonymous lady who secretly penned wildly romantic tales to enliven her quiet days. Yes, she would do very well. He remembered her as a romping lass, but he hadn't seen much of her during the two years since Meg's marriage and removal from the abbey. She was now suitably ladylike, with her prim lips and downcast eyes.

But when he put his plan to her, those modest eyes turned to dark and stormy cauldrons of wrath. "The authoress of *Chaos Is Come Again!*" she exclaimed. "I would not claim to have written such drivel for all the money in the mint. It is a horrid, silly story. I despised Eugenie."

He was abashed at her forthright condemnation. His pride felt a sting as well. It was one thing for the author to condemn it, but for a chit who lived with her nose in a marble-covered novel to show her contempt was doing it too brown. Surely *Chaos* was not that bad! Even as his resentment sizzled, his sharp mind took note that she had read it.

"I didn't realize you had set up as a critic, Sissie," he said through thin lips.

"I quit reading chapbooks some years ago, milord," she retorted.

"Who did write the book, and how does it come that you are seeking a lady to masquerade as its author, Montaigne?" Miss Caldwell asked, peering up from her stitchery.

"It was written by my aunt," he said, omitting any Christian name.

"Lady DeVigne!" Cicely exclaimed. "I don't believe it. She is much too sensible."

"No, not Lady DeVigne. Another aunt. Mama's spinster sister. From Cornwall," he added, to put a few hundred miles in the way of the young ladies' discovering that this aunt did not exist.

"Your mama is from Surrey," Cicely said at once.

"How does it come her unmarried sister has removed to Cornwall?"

Her question signaled him he must be a little more careful what lies he told. The Caldwells had been neighbors to the Montaignes for aeons. Sissie might be a young provincial, but she was sharp. "She was sent there as companion to an elderly relative several decades ago," he replied.

It was Miss Caldwell who first saw the advantage to the scheme of Cicely's going to London. "You would like to see Meg again, Cicely," Anne said. "And while it would be *acting* a lie, there is no real harm in it. It is the motive, you know, that constitutes the harm. The proceeds are to go to charity. You would meet Mr. Murray," she added with a meaningful glance at her sister.

Montaigne saw the flash of interest in Sissie's stormy eyes. Meg was right, then. Sissie was writing something herself. What on earth could she find to write about, living so cribbed and confined as she did? He began to outline the temptations inherent to a struggling writer in the visit.

"Mr. Murray has invited some of his writers to this dinner he has planned. A few of the literary reviews wish to interview the author as well."

Cicely considered the matter for about sixty seconds, then spoke. "I shall do it on one condition, Montaigne. You must allow me to show Mr. Murray my own book. He will pay some attention to it when he thinks I wrote *Chaos Is Come Again*. Not that the books are anything alike," she added indignantly.

Montaigne felt a spurt of interest to discover Sissie had finished a whole novel. He disliked the idea of her showing it to Murray under his auspices.

14

She would have written some dreadful, juvenile thing, but then Murray didn't know Montaigne had written *Chaos*. He looked at her firm chin and said, "I have no objection to it."

"What would I have to do, exactly?"

"Just go to Mr. Murray's dinner party at the Pulteney."

"Alone?" she asked, her eyes staring in horror.

"No, no. I would accompany you. Murray might wish to discuss your writing another book along the lines of *Chaos*. My aunt, of course, would write it. You have only to listen to him and agree. The critics will discuss literature a little, but then that will be no difficulty for an ardent reader like you."

She didn't catch the hint of sarcasm in his tone. "And it is for a good cause," she said, nodding.

He spoke on persuasively about the poor orphans, mentioning the sum the book had earned thus far.

"That much!" Cicely cried, her eyes opening wide. "Did you hear that, Anne? And to think that horrid Mr. Egerton wanted me to pay him two hundred pounds to print my book. Well, I shall ask Papa's permission," she said, but her sparkling eyes told Montaigne she was keen for the adventure.

Miss Caldwell cleared her throat. "I don't think that is such a good idea, Sissie. Papa might balk at the notion of your deceiving the public. It would be better to tell him only that Meg has invited you for a short visit. He will not mind that." She turned to Montaigne. "Mr. Murray does not plan to actually put Sissie's name on the next book?"

"No, no. He just wishes to meet her. The literary set in London will learn her identity, but there is a freemasonry among writers. When they discover she does not wish her identity known, they'll keep it to themselves."

"Papa has no dealings with them," Miss Caldwell said. "He'll never hear a whisper of it. I think you should do it, Sissie. How else are you going to meet the sort of people who could do your writing career some good? And your *Georgiana* is really a very good book." Anne looked hopefully at Montaigne.

If they asked him to read the book, he would have to say something nice about it. Perhaps Meg would read it for him.

"But if Papa does find out . . . ," Sissie said, and sat, worrying.

Miss Caldwell looked commandingly at Montaigne. "Then Lord Montaigne will do your explaining and apologizing for you."

Montaigne foresaw the difficulties in this scheme. He was the perpetrator of the idea; he was older, a gentleman. If anything went amiss, he could end up with a fine mess in his dish. Not that anything was likely to go amiss, but why take chances?

"No, I don't care for this underhanded business," he said firmly. "I shall speak to your papa and get his permission before you go. Where would I find him?"

"At the oast houses," Miss Caldwell said.

Montaigne left, and the two young ladies immediately began discussing the adventure.

"Papa will never let me go," Cicely said.

"Montaigne will turn him up sweet. The orphans, you know. Now, what we must decide is what you are to wear to this dinner party. How fortunate we put new ribbons on your blue ball gown last week for the winter assembly. You must take Mama's diamond necklace and my new fringed shawl. Meg will have a coiffeur in to do something stylish to your hair. Oh, I am so happy for you, Sissie. I know you will sell your book. You will be the next Frances Burney, mark my words."

"Hardly that famous!" Sissie demurred. "But it will be a wonderful opportunity for me to see how London Society goes on. I feel my writing is hampered by my lack of experience."

"Meg can help you there. Why, there is no saying who you will meet at her house. She is top of the trees. You might even meet an eligible *parti*," Miss Caldwell added with a teasing smile.

Cicely threw her head back and sighed luxuriously. "I don't care if I never marry, if only I can get my novel published. We will grow old together, Anne, you keeping house and me writing. I can't think of anything I should like better."

Anne looked at her askance. "I can! We have a pretty dull time here. I do think you might put just a little more romance in your next novel, Sissie. I'm not speaking of anything like that foolish Eugenie and her crystal tears and swoons, but perhaps a handsome hero and a slightly younger herione."

"You know you were my herione, Anne. I just added a decade to her age to fool the neighbors. I read in an article of advice to writers that we ought to write about what we know. What do I know about handsome heroes?"

"I know it was my story, my dear, and I am flattered that you see me in such a glow of admiration, but one book about me is enough. I should not mind in the least if you had given me a husband at the end, instead of consigning me to watching my nieces and nephews."

"It's not supposed to be a romance, Anne. It's about real life."

"There's such a thing as too much reality—in books, I mean. Romance is a part of life, too."

Cicely scowled. "I knew you liked Eugenie better than Georgiana."

"No, not better. Georgiana could have used just a touch of Eugenie's emotion, and Eugenie could have used a good deal of Georgiana's sound common sense. It might be interesting, in another book, to try a more varied cast of characters and a different background. That is why I think this trip to London will be such a help. London has everything from lords and heiresses to beggars and villains. You will see palaces as well as the worst slums there. I wonder how Georgiana would have behaved if she had been confronted with knaves and beggars, as Eugenie was, instead of safe, rural neighbors."

"At least she would not have bawled."

They were still discussing heroines and the visit to London when Lord Montaigne returned half an hour later. Before he could speak, Cicely jumped up. His dashing smile told her that her papa had agreed to the visit. It struck Sissie, who was always on the lookout for new characters, that Montaigne would make an interesting one. What a life he must lead! Tip of the ton, probably with mistresses and all sorts of ladies on the catch for him. And she would soon have a glimpse of his life, with all its glamour.

"You did it!" she cried, and ran forward to pitch herself into his arms. As Montaigne was a safe decade older than she and she had run tame at St. Albans Abbey forever, she felt no constraint until she felt his body stiffen. Over his shoulder, she saw Anne's startled face. Then Sissie backed off with a little blush and added, "You talked him into it! How did you do it, Lord Montaigne?" She added the "Lord" to lend an air of formality to her indiscretion.

"The orphans were helpful. So was the loan of my prize bull. He will be servicing Bessie when she is in season."

Montaigne would not have spoken so bluntly to ladies of the ton in London, but this plain talk caused no consternation to these farmer's daughters.

"And I will be going to London!" Cicely sighed. Her face wore the dazed look of a state lottery winner. "When shall we be leaving?"

"Tomorrow morning, as early as you can get yourself ready. Don't worry about gowns and things. Meg will give you a hand there. She's very eager to see you. I wish you could come as well, Anne, but I know you won't leave your papa alone—with only his valet and butler and cook and a houseful of servants to look after him," he added with a rueful smile.

"No, indeed. I am that indispensible creature, a widower's spinster daughter, and well enough satisfied with my fate. Will you have a glass of wine, milord?"

"I must be running along. I shall have a ride about the estate while I'm here." He turned to Cicely. "What time will you be ready to leave?"

"Is eight early enough?" she asked.

A tolerant smile moved his lips. "Nine will be fine. I don't want to rush you. Or myself," he added, under his breath. When he'd said "early," his hope was to get away by noon, but he appreciated the early start.

He took his leave of the ladies and drove on to the

abbey, well satisfied with his visit. Sissie's manners were rustic but rather charming. A London belle wouldn't have pitched herself into his arms in that hoydenish fashion. He remembered the sudden thrust of her full bosoms against his chest and the resulting heat that suddenly invaded him. Sissie had certainly grown up in a hurry. It seemed only yesterday that she and Meg had been young girls, tearing through the meadows and coming home in tatters from their encounters with nettles and briars.

He'd slip her the hint that pitching herself into a gentleman's arms was not the mode in London. A kiss on the cheek was the fashionable greeting.

He was happy for a restful evening without company, away from the turmoil of the House, and Society.

At Elmdale, delightful confusion reigned as the ladies rushed about, choosing gowns and bonnets and slippers. Mr. Caldwell asked Cicely into his study to warn her of the lack of morals that prevailed in London. His heart was not entirely made of flint, however. He also gave her fifty pounds, saying she might want to buy a new bonnet while she was there. In her reticule were another fifty pounds, the sum she and Anne had managed to scrape together between them, with some help from the housekeeping money.

The entire household came to the door the next morning to see Miss Cicely off in Montaigne's elegant black crested carriage with its four matched horses. While her small trunk and a gift to Lady Fairly of a peck of apples from Caldwell's orchard were stored in the carriage, Cicely took her farewell.

"I shan't forget to find you a pair of blue silk

stockings, Anne," she called. "And your graduated glass measuring vessel, Cook. I shall buy all the new fashion magazines, Anne, and take particular note of what sort of bonnets are the rage. Be sure to tell Miss Cooper why I cannot call on her this afternoon, for I told her I would. Good-bye, Papa."

Then she climbed into the carriage, where she immediately let down the window for another volley of noisy farewells. Montaigne did not try to hasten their departure. He smiled tolerantly at her excitement. This adventure would probably be the highlight of her life. Her debut and grand tour rolled into one. How her eyes sparkled! And what a healthy glow on her young cheeks. Probably the result of eating apples.

He busied himself with John Groom, trying to decide where to store the peck of apples. Obviously they could not be tied to the basket or the roof, or they would bounce all over the road. In the end, the apples were stored on the floor of the carriage, between him and Cicely.

At last they were off. After a few hundred yards, Cicely stopped waving out the window and was available for conversation.

"Are you much familiar with London?" Montaigne inquired, to get the conversational ball rolling.

"Oh yes, I know it like the palm of my hand. We used to go every year when Mama was alive, and twice since then. We stay at Reddishes Hotel. I have seen the mint, and the animals at Exeter Exchange, and Hyde Park and St. Paul's and everything."

"Ah, I see you are no tourist," he said, then felt foolish, as it was precisely the tourist attractions she had mentioned.

She took him up on it at once. "I am, really. Or

21

have been until now. I've never stayed in a house. What I want to see this time is the rest of London. You know, the places the ton frequent, in case I ever want to write about them. I am particularly interested in the slums," she added.

Lord Montaigne lifted his quizzing glass and studied her a moment. "I beg your pardon?"

"I said the slums. It's where the poor people live."

"I was not under the misapprehension that the ton lived there."

"And perhaps Bedlam," she added, unoffended.

"Where the lunatics live," he said.

"Just so. Anne feels my next novel should have a little more excitement in it."

"More like *Chaos*, in fact?" he inquired, arching a playful eyebrow at her. "So you have no objection to romance."

"That's not what I meant at all. *Chaos* was more fairy tale than romance. It leads ordinary girls astray to imagine a white knight, all full of virtue, is going to marry them. More likely to debauch them. It makes them dissatisfied with the ordinary sort of man they might actually land. One not likely to be a lord, with a face like a Greek god and all the virtues of the twelve apostles on his broad shoulders."

"Ravencroft was not described as like a Greek god."

"No, but it was there, between the lines. Now that I know your elderly aunt from Cornwall wrote the book, I can understand why it is so unrealistic. It's an old lady's idea of romance, dreamed up in her loneliness and embroidered while she sat alone, perhaps remembering some lover from her youth."

The young provincial's condescension grated on Montaigne's nerves. "The critics felt the heroine was particularly well drawn," he mentioned. Cicely's answer was a snort of derision.

"You have some experience in romance, I take it?"

"Of course I have. I'm twenty years old. I've had two offers."

"As you apparently refused them, there cannot have been much romance involved."

"You're very much mistaken, milord. I was totally infatuated with Sir William Sykes. My heart was quite cracked when Papa rejected him. It turned out he hadn't a feather to fly with, and he dressed as fine as ninepence. But I didn't go into a decline—or swoon, or even cry much—except the day he left for London."

"What *did* you do?" he asked with mild interest. There might be a sequel to *Chaos*. He was interested to learn from an avid reader.

"Anne gave me her second-best bonnet and a box of bonbons. I ate the bonbons and was sick to my stomach. I felt much better in the morning. We went into town and bought new ribbons for the bonnet so everyone wouldn't recognize it."

"Very romantic!" he said with a jeering look.

"Better than going into a decline. Life's too short to waste in tears. But it is mainly bored ladies who read a book like *Chaos*. I daresay your aunt wanted them to identify with Eugenie. What she ought to have done was set her book in the Middle Ages. That would have lent it at least a modicum of credibility. No lady today would behave as Eugenie did."

"Yet she appealed to several thousand of today's readers."

"To simpleminded readers. Cook read the book to the servants. They all enjoyed it very much."

Montaigne could find no reply to this piece of

condescension except to remark that he had seen it on the sofa table of many ladies of fashion. A chit hardly out of the schoolroom, who imagined she knew London like the palm of her hand because she had visited St. Paul's, had undertaken to malign his extremely popular novel—and he could not even give her the setdown she deserved.

"As you are to pose as the author, it will perhaps be best if you not bring your powerful critical analysis to bear on it in public, Miss Cicely," he said stiffly.

She gave him an avuncular pat on the arm. "Don't worry, Montaigne. I shall simper and smile and pretend to be vastly pleased with myself. But *entre nous*, we both know it is a perfectly *horrid* book."

Montaigne lifted an apple from the peck and bit into it with a snap, to keep himself from a rude retort. He saw that the next few days were going to be even more trying than he had anticipated.

Chapter Three

"So this is where Meg lives," Cicely said when the carriage drew to a stop in front of an impressive mansion on Berkeley Square. Her tone lacked enthusiasm. "We heard at home that Lord Fairly was very well to grass. This is nothing compared to your abbey, Montaigne."

He felt again that surge of annoyance. "You will find that London mansions are considerably smaller than country estates. Land here is at a premium."

"I didn't expect him to grow oats in his backyard, but I thought the house itself would be grander. I'll make a note of what you said."

When she was admitted by a snooty butler, Cicely saw at once that while the house was smaller than an abbey, it was not a whit less grand. Any part of the entrance hall that was not marble was either carved, coffered, or gilded. At the end of the hall, a horseshoe staircase formed a graceful semicircle, with a banistered corridor above. The staircase was carpeted in crimson, with a white marble handrail and ornate brass spindles.

"Why does such a small house have two front staircases?" she asked Montaigne.

"They are like the flowers on a lady's bonnet—for looks, not function."

"It does look very stylish," she allowed.

Lady Fairly heard their arrival and came darting to greet them. She looked at Cicely in her country outfit, with her hair pulled back under an unfashionable bonnet, gawking around like the veriest hick. Gracious! She had forgotten how countrified the Caldwells were. Sissie, undismayed, ran forward and threw her arms around Meg.

"Sissie, how lovely to see you," Meg said when she had struggled free. "How are all the folks at Elmdale?"

"Pretty well, thanks. They send their love. Papa's gout has been at him. Did I tell you Anne has put on her caps? I've heard of ladies leaping at the altar, but to be leaping at the shelf is just nonsense. I don't think she's given up on finding a match entirely. She wants me to buy her a pair of blue silk stockings to go with her new gown. We read in *La Belle Assemblée* that colored stockings to match the gown are all the crack."

She peeled off her own mantle and bonnet as she spoke, and handed them to the butler.

"How are you, Meg?" she inquired, casting a long look on her old friend. "You look a little peaked. Are you enceinte yet? That will often lend an air of fatigue."

Lady Fairly felt that same sort of annoyance that had been plaguing her brother throughout the trip.

"No, not yet," she said, forcing a smile.

"Pity. You and Lord Fairly must be growing impatient. But I daresay you will find yourself in the family way soon. You really ought to take better care of yourself. You look hagged."

"It's the late nights that have destroyed my complexion," Lady Fairly replied, darting a glance in

26

the closest mirror. Mirrors were plentiful in the beauty's mansion. As she observed her reflection next to Sissie Caldwell's, she was struck with the difference in their appearance. She was the same age as Sissie, yet she looked a decade older. Sissie still had the full, pink cheek and glossy eye of youth.

"Why do you stay up so late?" Cicely asked.

"We go out a good deal. Do come in and have a glass of wine."

Cicely turned a critical eye on the saloon as she entered, taking notice of the rich appointments, all to be recorded in her notebook for future use. Was it possible she counted a dozen lamps in one room? "Could I have tea instead?" she asked.

"Certainly. Coddle, tea for Miss Cicely."

"And some biscuits, if it's not too much trouble. I am famished. I was so excited I couldn't eat a bite of breakfast. Montaigne had an apple en route. Papa sent a peck of apples. You always said our apples made a better tart than those from the abbey, though they're a little sour to eat out of hand. You might want to make a tart the next time you have a dinner party."

"How nice. Thank you," Lady Fairly said, casting a speaking glance to her brother. Apple tart indeed! As if she would serve such a thing to her guests—though she wouldn't mind having Cook make her up one for her own private treat.

They took up seats by the blazing grate.

"This is a lovely little house, Meg," Cicely said.

"My dining room seats two dozen, and the ballroom can hold over a hundred," Lady Fairly replied.

"I've been explaining to Sissie that London residences are smaller than country estates," Montaigne said, swallowing a smile.

27

"Monty has told me why you are here," Lady Fairly said, hoping to deflect the conversation from further aspersions on her mansion and her person. In particular, she disliked the way Sissie kept studying her face.

"I'm happy to oblige him. It will be great fun to meet other writers."

"Then you have written something?" Lady Fairly asked with mild interest.

"Yes, a novel. A serious novel, not a ludicrous thing like your aunt's book. I hope Mr. Murray doesn't think I can write nothing but potboilers."

The brother and sister exchanged another of those speaking looks.

"It is the potboilers that keep the publisher solvent," Montaigne told her. Then he turned to Meg. "Unlike the rest of Society, Sissie doesn't care for our aunt's book."

"I thought it was excellent," Lady Fairly said, as much from anger as conviction, though she had enjoyed it.

Cicely laughed merrily. "You always had wretched taste in novels, Meg. Do you still read those things from the Minerva Press?"

"Certainly not," she replied, shoving her current marble cover under a cushion. "And furthermore, you are the one who introduced me to them, Sissie."

"When we were youngsters," Sissie said. She saw the familiar marble cover sticking out from behind a cushion. Her instinct was to make fun of Meg. She happened to catch Montaigne's eye. He was watching her like a hawk. She decided to show him she could be discreet when necessary and said nothing.

The tea tray eventually arrived. As Coddle had

brought three cups, they all had tea. Sissie also ate several biscuits and a slice of bread and butter.

"I had best not eat any more or I shall spoil my lunch," she said, looking hungrily at the bread.

"And your figure," Meg added playfully.

"True. It's you who should eat something. You look like a scarecrow." Then she gasped in shame. "Not an ugly scarecrow, Meg. I just meant you're so thin. Perhaps that's why you can't get pregnant."

"I've only been married two years!"

"You must be at your wits' end." When this elicited no reply, Sissie said, "What time do you eat your meals? Do you take dinner at six, or a fashionable seven?"

"Seven or eight, depending on whether we plan to go out, but we shall have some luncheon in a few hours."

"A few hours! Then I shall have some more bread," Cicely said and picked up another slice. She looked for cold mutton, but found none. "Anne hoped you might know a coiffeur who could do something with my hair," was her next comment.

"Yes, I have been thinking I must smarten you up," Lady Fairly replied, happy to be able to retaliate for earlier slights. "No one would believe my cousin would wear such a gown," she added.

"Naturally I shan't wear this to the dinner party. Fortunately, I had just put new bows on my ball gown, and Anne lent me Mama's diamonds."

"New bows, eh?" Montaigne said. "That should do the trick."

He finished up his tea and rose to take his leave. "I leave you in Meg's capable hands, Sissie. I shall call on you tomorrow."

"Oh, good. I want to see the slums."

29

"Where the poor people live," Montaigne explained to Meg, with a glint of mischief in his eye. "Perhaps Meg could take you. I am very busy at the House. I meant I would drop in for a moment in the afternoon to arrange details for the evening dinner party."

Lady Fairly gave him a gimlet glance. "What are you doing this evening, Monty? I'm sure you would like to take Sissie with you."

"There is an evening sitting in the House," he lied. "But no doubt Sissie would be happy to do whatever you are doing."

Sissie looked expectantly to her hostess.

"I thought Sissie and I would have a nice cose this afternoon. I'm attending the theater this evening. The Montagues invited Fairly and me to join them, along with the Wartons."

This told Montaigne that the six seats in the box would be filled, leaving Sissie alone. It was obviously ineligible to treat a young lady who was doing him a favor so shabbily.

"Ah, just so. I believe I shall skip tonight's sitting and also attend the theater. Sissie, would you like to come with me?"

Cicely looked uncertain. "Should I not go with Meg?" she asked.

"Meg will have you all to herself until after dinner. I insist you come with me. I shan't keep you up late."

"Share and share alike," Lady Fairly said, happy to have fobbed her guest off for one evening. "We shall expect you around eight, Monty."

"Until then." He bowed to the ladies and left.

As soon as the bread and biscuits were gone, the ladies went abovestairs to discuss the important matter of toilette. Cicely gaped in pleasure at her room, which looked like something out of a fairy tale, with its delicate white French furnishings and its gleaming lutestring canopy and drapes in a dusty rose shade.

"How lovely! I feel like a princess."

"I decorated it myself," Lady Fairly said. "You know I always liked rose."

"It's just as I imagined," Sissie said, rushing around the room and examining details. Lady Fairly looked at her with something like satisfaction.

Cicely's trunk had been unpacked while she was belowstairs. She went to the clothespress and proudly displayed her Olympian blue ball gown, with the new bows added. Lady Fairly did not gasp in consternation, but she had to work to control her face. She would not be caught dead in a ditch in such an unfashionable gown, nor did she relish any guest of hers being seen in such an outfit. The material, the cut, the surfeit of bows—it fairly shrieked "country."

Cicely saw her hostess's dismay and said, "I daresay it's too fancy for the theater. I had planned to wear it to Mr. Murray's dinner party, with Mama's diamond necklace."

"Much too fancy," Lady Fairly said. "But it is no matter. My closet is bulging. You must wear something of mine. We are not that different in size. I have lost a little weight, but the gowns from my trousseau will fit you. Come, let us have a look."

When they went to Lady Fairly's room, Cicely was momentarily stunned into silence. "Oh, Meg! What a perfectly lavish room!" she cried, when she found tongue. "Anne was right. This trip is very broadening for me. I never would have thought anyone but a princess lived like this, and with a whole cosmetics counter to herself."

She went to the toilet table and began lifting the chased silver lids on a set of crystal containers to peer and sniff into them. "What are all these enchanting things?"

"Why, they are my scent bottles and powders and rouge."

"Rouge!" Cicely laughed aloud. "You don't mean you paint your face!"

"When I am looking peaky. Everyone does it."

"I shall make a note of that as well. Gracious, you've turned into a fine lady, and never writing a word about it to me, while I kept you up to date about every little thing."

Lady Fairly felt a trifle guilty on this score. She murmured something about being so busy and hastened to find a new distraction. "My gowns are in here," she said, moving to the side of the room where a matching pair of oversize armoires stood, filling the wall. She drew open one door and gestured at the gowns.

Cicely stared for a long moment before speaking. "I had thought Fairly must be poor when I saw your little house, but now that I have seen how elegant everything is, and how many gowns you have, I believe he must be a millionaire."

Lady Fairly glowed in pleasure. She was the sort who could take any amount of admiration but very little criticism. She began to look on her old friend more warmly. She rifled through the gowns, finally drawing one out. It was Italian silk, in her favorite pale dusty rose shade, cut very low at the bodice, with a ruched skirt, each ruche fastened with a silk rosebud.

Cicely gazed in wonder, touching the dress lightly with her fingers, as if it might vanish at her touch. "It's the most beautiful thing I've ever seen in my life," she said in an awed voice. "I wouldn't dare to wear it. I would be bound to spill something on it and destroy it."

"No matter if you do. It's too large for me nowadays. Come to the mirror and hold it up in front of you." Cicely did as she was ordered. "There, it will look better on you than it did on me. Your darker hair sets it off. Fairly says my delicate coloring looks best in richer shades for evening wear."

"I wish I could have my portrait done, to show Anne. She would never believe it. Where did you find such a heavenly gown?"

"I have a French modiste. She's rather good."

"She's a wizard. May I try it on?"

"It will fit. We were the same size when I got married. We should have it pressed. The skirt is a little wrinkled from hanging in the closet for twelve months."

Meg pulled the bell cord and her dresser, a stern-looking woman of middle years, came in from the adjoining room. "Have this pressed, Perkins, and lay out my blue gown for this evening."

The dresser took the gown away. Cicely said, "Do you mind if I go to my room to make a few notes, Meg? I want to jot down all the new things I've learned today while they're fresh in my mind. I should like to make you the heroine of my next novel."

Meg's eyes lit up in delight. "Me! Good gracious, what have I ever done to deserve a book about me?"

"I want a new sort of heroine."

"I am hardly that," Meg said modestly.

"What I mean is a spoiled, rich beauty who has too much of everything, and idles her life away." A faraway look seized her lively face as she continued. "She is cold and barren, which will cause her husband to look elsewhere for amusement."

"Thank you very much!" Meg exclaimed, fire in her eyes.

"Oh, but that is just the beginning. Before the end, I'll put her through her paces and she'll come to her senses. I always like a happy ending. And besides, I shan't call her Meg. No one will know it's based on you."

"I don't see the point of my being the heroine, if no one is to know." Meg damped down her annoyance. She must be polite to this farouche creature, for Monty's sake. "I have a megrim. I shall lie down until lunchtime. Make yourself at home, Sissie. I shall send a girl to help you with your toilette for this evening."

"You don't have to do that, but if you could help me dress my hair, I should be happy for it."

"I do not dress hair. We 'spoiled beauties' have a woman to do that for us. I'll send Perkins to you. Lunch is at two. If you're hungry in the meanwhile, you must feel free to ask for a snack," she said rather tartly. "And now I shall leave you."

"I'm sorry if I offended you, Meg," Cicely said in a small voice.

"You didn't offend me. You know nothing about how the ton live," she said, and bowed her guest stiffly out of the door. She then threw herself on the bed and reviewed the insults she had endured from Sissie Caldwell. Calling her a scarecrow, denigrating one of the finest mansions in London! Really, the chit was impossible! Sissie had always been outspoken, of course. Meg rose from the bed and went to her mirror. She *was* looking rather hagged. She remembered Sissie's vibrant cheeks and sparkling eyes. Was it her diet that was preventing Meg from giving Fairly a pledge of her love? It certainly wasn't for lack of trying in the beginning, but lately Fairly's ardor had cooled.

Cicely realized she had gotten off on a bad foot and was sorry for it, but overall she was satisfied with the visit thus far. She had found her new heroine and was already envisaging sending her to the slums of London to learn a few things about real life. Meg was quite right: Cicely knew nothing about how the ton lived, but she was fast learning. She knew that her old friend had changed, and for the worse. She looked hagged, despite her rouge pot. She obviously squandered a fortune on her clothes. It was odd that a young bride had not given her husband of two years a single baby yet. How had Meg changed so much in two short years? There were mysteries to be plumbed in wicked London, and Cicely could hardly wait to begin plumbing.

Chapter Four

"I cannot be seen in public in this gown! I'm half naked!" Cicely exclaimed when Meg stopped at her room to take her down to dinner. Cicely lifted her hands to her bodice to cover her shame. But as she looked to Meg, she saw that her hostess's gown was of the same cut. Meg's bosoms were not so full as her own, however. Hers seemed to be rising out of the gown like yeast bread rising in the pan.

"It is what everyone will be wearing," Meg said, casting a jealous eye on those full young breasts. "If you're not comfortable, wear a shawl."

Cicely snatched up Meg's white woolen shawl.

"Good God, not that blanket! I brought you this one that goes with the rose gown." She handed Cicely an elegant paisley shawl with a silk fringe.

Cicely draped it around her shoulders and folded it over the top of her gown. "I don't see how I can eat with this on."

"I'm sure you'll manage," Meg said rather astringently. Cicely had certainly put away a good luncheon. "I see Perkins has fixed up your hair. Very nice." She peered to see how that cluster of curls had been arranged. It looked quite striking. Sissie had rich, glossy hair the color of a peeled chestnut.

"We practiced while you paid that duty visit to

Fairly's aunt this afternoon. Perkins had to use eight pins and two combs. I'll have the megrims before the evening is over."

"Beauty does not come cheap. The price includes suffering. You might put that in your book, Sissie." The price also included a quick visit to the chemist's shop that afternoon for a bottle of tonic guaranteed to put the roses back in Meg's cheeks. The visit to Aunt Fairly was merely the pretext.

"It's a good thing beauty is a luxury," Sissie said. "A lady need only suffer as much as she wants to. For myself, I'd as lief be plain. But not in London, of course," she added.

Lord Fairly was waiting on nettles to greet Miss Cicely. There was little of more interest to him than a young lady. He had met Sissie at his wedding at the abbey. Wildly infatuated with his bride at the time, he had not paid much heed to the local beauties. His practiced eye now told him he had missed out on a prime chick. Miss Cicely was something special. Her luxuriant curls, arranged in a fashionable flounce on top of her head, provided a dramatic contrast to her peaches-and-cream complexion. And the eyes! Lord, they were like stormy lakes. He suspected there might be an interesting body as well beneath the shawl she clutched around her.

"So this is little Sissie Caldwell!" he said, deciding to call her Sissie from the beginning, to hasten things along. "A pleasure to see you again, Sissie. By Jove, you look splendid. You will take the shine out of them all. Kind of you to spare us a few days."

Sissie had already been warned that Lord Fairly did not know the whole of why she was in London. He thought she had actually written *Chaos Is Come Again*, and while he had not read it, he knew it was a great success. It seemed strange to Cicely that Meg should keep secrets from her husband, but Meg made little of it.

"It is kind of you to have me, milord," she said, making her best curtsy.

"Time for something wet before dinner, eh, Meg?" he said, reaching for the sherry decanter.

While he poured the drink, Cicely settled in to observe a Society couple at home. She was familiar with Fairly's appearance—tall, slender, blond, blue-eyed, and handsome, with more the air of a dandy than a Corinthian. His blue velvet jacket nipped in a little too tightly about his waist and bulged suspiciously large at the shoulders. His cravat, too, was larger and more intricate than the norm. He fiddled with a quizzing glass that hung on a black cord. He left off playing with it only to draw out a snuff box. He made a great business of taking snuff.

Fairly's appearance had not changed, but Cicely found his manners less pleasing than before. He hardly glanced at Meg, nor did he compliment her on her lovely gown. Meg seemed equally disinterested in her husband. She didn't ask him if he had had a good day, as Cicely and Anne always inquired of Papa, even if they knew he had only been out checking up on his hops. They all sat down for a glass of sherry.

"Did you have a good day, Lord Fairly?" Sissie inquired, to give Meg the hint she had forgotten.

"Dash it, call me Fairly," was his reply. "Meg tells me Monty has stolen you away from us for Murray's dinner party tomorrow evening. Demmed shame. I should like to take you to a ball. 'Pon my word, I believe Monty has his eye on this little lady, Meg."

"Don't be an ass," Meg said.

Cicely stared in consternation. Was it possible she had timed her visit during a lovers' quarrel?

Fairly ignored the insult entirely. "At least we shall all be at the theater this evening."

"Sissie is going with Monty," Meg said.

"Pity. Ah well, it's impossible to talk at the theater anyhow. We shall all get together for a tidy little dinner after at the Clarendon."

"Will it not be late by the time the play is over?" Sissie asked.

"Devil a bit of it. If we eat up our mutton quickly, we might catch a few dances at some do or other as well."

Cicely thought a play and dinner were quite enough for one evening, but as a guest, she didn't say so. She was beginning to understand why Meg looked so hagged.

Fairly continued, "I'll tell you what we'll do. Tomorrow I shall take you on the strut on Bond Street, stop at Hyde Park to show you off. And you too, Meg," he added as an afterthought.

Meg displayed no interest in the outing. "In November? No, I thank you. Sissie mentioned wanting blue stockings."

"Blue stockings, eh?" Fairly smiled, trying for a glimpse of the ankle he assumed they would adorn. "I hope that don't mean you are a bluestocking, Sissie. One of those dashed clever ladies who speaks Latin, what?"

"No indeed. The stockings are for my sister. I assure you I don't know Latin. What I should like to do tomorrow is to see the slums," she said. She felt uncomfortable with Fairly looking at her in that strange, leering way, which she kindly attributed to

39

an excess of wine. She suspected the glass he held was not the first one he had indulged in.

"Ha-ha! Slums. By Jove, you are an Original, Miss Sissie. We can do better than that."

"But I particularly want to see the slums."

His eyes opened wide in horror. "Good God! You ain't a do-gooder, I hope?"

"It is research for a novel," his wife informed him.

"But no one wants to read about slums," he said. "It don't do to make a fuss about that sort of thing. A friend of Hannah More, are you?"

"I have never met her," Cicely assured him. "I don't write about religion."

"Thank God for that. Too much religion around to suit me. It is well enough for the ladies; Sunday gives a man enough religion to last the week. Slums, eh? Well, why not, if it would please you."

It was a relief when dinner was announced. Cicely was busy making a mental inventory of the courses and removes. She also noticed that both Fairlys enjoyed a fairly liquid dinner. They drank more than they ate, which was strange, because dinner was a veritable feast. It proved impossible to wield her knife and fork without letting go of her shawl. Fairly noticed it and smiled in satisfaction. With his wife at the end of the table, he didn't say anything, but he was busy composing compliments to be delivered on a more convenient occasion.

Of course he realized that he couldn't seduce a young lady under his own roof, nor did he particularly want to. Appearance counted for a good deal with him. He liked to be seen about town with beautiful women. It flattered his vanity to do so, since he had so few other claims to fame. His empty nursery was a constant slur on his manhood.

As soon as dinner was over, Montaigne called for Cicely. He blinked to see such a stylish young lady waiting for him. Meg's servants had worked wonders to turn Cicely into a fashion doll.

"Very nice, Sissie," he said, his eyes traveling slowly from the tip of her chestnut curls to her kid slippers.

"Don't look so shocked, Montaigne," she said pertly. "It's still me under all the fine feathers. Meg fixed me up. Don't I look nice?"

"Charming, but as you have expressed an interest in learning your way about Society, I shall risk offending you and say that even an Incomparable does not crow over her own beauty."

"No need to take a huff. It's only the gown I meant."

"The gown never looked lovelier," Fairly said, with no notion of offending its former wearer.

As there was no time to spare, they all left at once. Fairly's carriage led off.

"How is the visit going so far?" Montaigne asked when he and Cicely were settled in his carriage.

"It's been an eye-opener. I had no idea the ton lived the way they do."

"Is Fairly pestering you?" He hadn't thought Fairly would be interested in Sissie, but of course that was before Meg had turned her into a dasher.

Her blunt "He's an ass" reassured Montaigne that Cicely was in no danger from Fairly. "Meg said so herself, so I am only agreeing with her."

"The sort of ass who likes pretty ladies."

"Is there a sort of man who doesn't? That's only natural—as long as he keeps within bounds."

"And does he keep within bounds?"

"I'm not sure what the boundaries are in London."

Then she looked at him in alarm. "Good gracious, I hope you're not suggesting he might molest me?"

"I would not use such a harsh word as 'molest.'"

"That's a relief. I feared I would have to push my dresser in front of my bedroom door at night. It wouldn't surprise me much if he tried to get me behind a door to sneak a kiss. I'll yell my head off if he tries that. Are he and Meg on the outs? They hardly said a word during dinner."

With a memory of countless dull dinners at the Fairlys', Montaigne replied, "No. When they come to cuffs, Meg takes her meals in her room."

They drove on awhile in silence. Montaigne was reassured by Cicely's sensible plan if Fairly tried any tricks. At the theater, he stopped to greet a few guests and present Cicely to them. When they entered their box, Cicely was surprised to see Fairly and Meg ensconced there, along with the Montagues.

"I had a word with the page," Fairly explained. "Since there were only the two of you in the box, we decided to join you."

"But what of the Wartons?" Cicely asked, startled at such casual treatment of friends.

"They invited the Sinclairs to take our seats," Meg said. "The Sinclairs had come alone. Their guests begged off at the last minute."

Cicely was familiar with the grandeur of the theater from her one visit to the Christmas pantomime, but she had never attended in the evening before. The candlelight, the glitter of jewels on marble throats, the raised fans and opera glasses were all noted. There was a greater feeling of excitement than in daytime. The ladies were given the seats at the front of the box, the better to ogle the audience.

She took particular note of the ladies' conversation and was shocked by it.

"I see Lord Kingsley is with his wife, for a change," Lady Montague said. "He will send her straight home after, of course, and go to dinner with his *chère amie*. I don't know why Lady Kingsley puts up with it. I really don't."

"The reason is pretty obvious," Meg replied. "That's a new set of diamonds she's wearing."

Lady Montague lifted her opera glasses and studied the diamonds. "So it is. How does he afford it? He gave his light-skirt a set of emeralds last week."

"They say he has squandered his wife's portion as well as his own."

"Then his wife must find herself a wealthy patron," Lady Montague said. The ladies joined in a cynical little laugh.

Montaigne, listening from behind, was not shocked by the conversation, but it struck him that it would certainly sound outrageous to a simple country girl like Sissie. In fact, it was outrageous, and her pursed lips told him she was soaking in every scandalous word.

The play was to be *King Lear*. Cicely thought that serious tragedy merited discussion. To her amazement, just as the curtain was opening, Lady Montague asked, "What are we seeing tonight, Meg? Do you know?"

Meg had no idea. She inquired of her husband, who was equally ignorant. The play, for them, was not a place to see Shakespeare performed, but for them to be seen. It was Montaigne who knew the play. When Meg was told, she groaned.

"Not Shakespeare! What a bore."

Cicely met Montaigne's eye and just shook her head.

The ladies amused themselves during boring *King Lear* by ogling the gentlemen in nearby boxes and perusing the audience to see who was there. They poked each other in the ribs and chattered about what the ladies were wearing. They were the first ones to leave their box at the intermission and the last ones to return. During their promenade, they were greeted by a dozen rakes and rattles. Lady Fairly presented them all to her guest. Cicely didn't even attempt to take part in the conversation, but she stored it all up for consideration later.

She could hardly credit that her old friend had sunk so deeply into vice. In her opinion, the talk went beyond broad to encroach on the licentious. Montaigne had some thought of rescuing her, but she had come to London to learn, and he would let her learn the wicked truth about Society. He looked forward to hearing her views during the second intermission. Before he could approach her, that jackanapes Fairly was at her side and swept her away for a promenade along the corridor.

"We ought to bring Meg with us. Some of those gentlemen are not at all the thing, milord," Montaigne heard her say.

Then he was accosted by Lady Dearborne and forgot about Sissie.

"Demme, I wish you would call me Fairly," Fairly said to Cicely.

"What about Meg?" As she looked around, she saw one of the rakes had his arm around her waist.

"Meg can take care of herself. She has no need of me."

"Have you two had a falling-out, milord? I don't

44

mean to be a Nosey Parker, but Meg is my best friend, you must know. I couldn't help but notice you two don't behave as you used to."

Fairly was perfectly aware of the value of sympathy from a young lady. He played the role of wronged husband to the hilt. "She has no time for me, now that she has garnered her own court around her. I am good only for paying the bills. And they are mighty steep bills, too, I can tell you."

"Oh, dear! Why do you not talk to her, milord?"

"I have tried a dozen times. We only end up coming to cuffs. I have given up trying. We are virtually strangers."

"So that is why she has not become enceinte!"

Fairly cast his eyes down and tried to look heartbroken. "Things are not as I would wish. I am happy you have come, Sissie."

"I'll try to talk some sense into her."

"I fear that is a vain hope, but it will do me a world of good to have a sympathetic someone, an old friend, in whom I can confide my misery."

As Fairly hardly knew her, Cicely assumed it was in her capacity as his wife's old friend that he was confiding such intimate sorrows to her. It seemed her novel was writing itself. Her hero's hair changed from black to blond on the spot, and a new character was added to the plot. The heroine and hero must have a close friend who would act as solver of their marital woes. But first the friend had to discover the exact nature of their differences.

"I want you to tell me all about it, Fairly," she said, holding his hand and gazing soulfully into his eyes. "I shall stand by you and try to bring Meg to her senses. And since you have confided in me, I shall take advantage of a friend's prerogative and

45

suggest that you are not totally innocent, either. You drink a deal too much and are not at all considerate of Meg."

Fairly blinked in astonishment. This blunt stating of the truth with the bark on it was not what he expected or wanted.

"Demme, I am only drowning my sorrows," he protested.

Cicely gave him a chiding smile. "That is for cowards, sir. I expect a more manly response from Lord Fairly. Sorrows are not kittens, after all, that are so easily disposed of. I'm sorry to speak so bluntly, but sympathy doesn't butter any parsnips. We must get to the root of the problem."

Montaigne, watching from the sidelines, disliked to see Sissie holding Fairly's hands. That wretched Fairly was taking advantage of her. He took a deep breath to calm his nerves, excused himself from his companion, and headed toward them.

When Cicely spotted his advance, she said hastily, "We shall speak of this again. Let us go back to our box now."

Fairly turned away to greet some other friends. It was Montaigne who accompanied Cicely to the box.

"I see the jackass continues to bray loud and long," he said, hoping to hear what she had been discussing with Fairly.

"Even a jackass can have cause for complaint," was her unsatisfactory reply.

"It looked remarkably like flirtation from where I was standing."

"When did you have time to notice? You were flirting your head off with that fat lady in the puce gown."

"Lady Dearborne is not fat!"

"Oh, pardon me. That well-padded lady in the ugly puce gown. Married, I assume, as you call her Lady Dearborne? Not that that would make a hap'orth of difference at Vanity Fair."

"You are mistaken. It makes a good deal of difference. Until a young lady is married, she must behave with circumspection."

"Is that a dig at me and Fairly?"

"If the shoe fits . . ."

As they then met up with the Montagues, Cicely was unable to give him a setdown.

When the play resumed, Fairly thought over what Cicely had said, not with any view to improving his behavior, but to inventing ruses to engage her sympathy. He considered places they could go together to enjoy a flirtation without jeopardizing her reputation—though still enhancing his own. This visit to the slums had potential. He might arrange for some ruffians to accost them. He could play the hero, safe in the knowledge that the pistol pointed at them was not loaded. It would do his flagging reputation the world of good for a tale like that to make the rounds. Yes, by Jove, the future looked bright.

When the play was over, the party went to the Clarendon Hotel for a sumptuous dinner. Montaigne sat on Cicely's right side. Fairly managed to grab the seat on her left and spent a good deal of time gazing into her eyes and murmuring out his troubles, especially when Meg carried on with Lord Montague.

Montaigne found he could hardly get a word in edgewise. His temper began to fray. He was not accustomed to being ignored when he took a young lady out, yet to compete for her attention with

Fairly was beneath his dignity. He set up a flirtation with Mrs. Warton instead.

Cicely found it all very grand and very decadent—and very useful research—but her eyelids were becoming too heavy to take much note of things. She was extremely tired after her long day and wanted only to return to her lovely bedroom and go to sleep.

When the dinner was finally over, it was one-thirty. She could hardly believe it when Meg said, "Where shall we go now? If we hurry, we can catch a few dances at some ball or rout."

"It is very late," Cicely said, suppressing a yawn.

"If you're tired, Monty will take you home," Meg said.

"But I wanted a waltz with you, Sissie," Fairly pouted.

"Try waltzing with your wife," Montaigne said. "I am taking Sissie home."

Chapter Five

"Thank you, Montaigne," Cicely said, as he led her out to his carriage. "I am burned to the socket. How hard you members of the ton trot, in your vain search for pleasure."

"Spoken like a true philistine," he laughed. "But I think you enjoyed the evening. At least Fairly's braying, to judge by your enthusiastic attention."

"It's not every day I get to see a lord flirting. He's pretty smooth."

Montaigne's jaw muscles tensed in annoyance. He had already felt apprehensive to see how Meg had rigged Cicely out in the highest kick of fashion. Her appearance suggested a woman of the world—and Fairly was making a spectacle of himself over the chit. This was not at all what Montaigne had had in mind in bringing her to London. As the dinner party was tomorrow evening, however, it hardly seemed worthwhile making a fuss over it. She would be posted back to Elmdale within forty-eight hours.

"New fodder for your writing," he said.

"I appreciated the experience of attending the theater in the evening. It was enlightening," she allowed.

"Yes, one doesn't get that sort of performance in the provinces," he said with satisfaction.

"No indeed, for when we provincials attend the theater, the performance is limited to the stage. I shall not trespass so far on the truth as to say I enjoyed *King Lear*, for I scarcely heard a word of it. I fear Meg has changed since leaving the abbey."

"Things are different in London."

"They certainly are. Do you realize Fairly and Meg are practically on the verge of breaking up?"

"What are you talking about?" he demanded.

"Fairly says she doesn't understand him, and I believe he is right; or worse, she understands and doesn't give a tinker's curse. She thinks of nothing but gowns and balls and those horrid rattles who were surrounding her at the play. Now she has run off to dance until dawn. No wonder she looks so hagged, if she is up this late every night."

"Things will quiet down when winter sets in. The Fairlys will go to their estate in the country for Christmas, as they did last year."

"Much good that will do if they're estranged. Fairly is very eager to set up his nursery. You're a man of the world, Montaigne. I don't have to tell you why it is still empty after two years. They're not sleeping together."

"Good Lord!" Montaigne exclaimed. His shock had as much to do with Cicely's blunt speech as with the trouble between Meg and Fairly. He was aware that the first bloom had faded from the romance. Like most married members of the ton, the Fairlys each went their own way a good deal of the time, but Montaigne hadn't realized the situation had reached this state. Nor did he like that Sissie had taken Fairly's side in the matter.

"Your sister wants a good talking-to," she advised him. "I think it would come better from you than from me. The fact is, I think Meg doesn't care for me as much as she used to. She acts stiffish with me."

"You have decided Meg is the culprit, have you? Is that why you allowed Fairly to monopolize you all evening?"

"Better his company than those lechers Meg was with, since my escort decided to flirt with the fat— the lady in the puce gown. One of those lechers put his hand on my bottom. But I don't mean to say the fault is all Meg's by a long chalk. I told Fairly he drank too much and was inconsiderate. I plan to straighten him out, but Meg's reformation must come from you."

Montaigne didn't know whether to laugh or box her ears. That indignant remark about a hand on her bottom jerked at his funny bone, but of course it was farouche of her to mention it to him. He did not really object to her denigrating her hostess and delivering a lecture to her host, but when she complained of her escort being careless, when he had tried in vain to be with her, that was doing it too brown.

"You aren't going to singlehandedly change Society in two days, Sissie. You will find your short visit goes more smoothly if you confine your activities to being the author of the novel," he said. "As to that gown . . . I have told Murray you're a provincial lady. He is not expecting a high flier."

"Is that how I look?" she asked, pleased as punch with the accusation. "It's strange, is it not, that all the old clichés are true. In a simple sort of way, clothes *do* make the lady. I never had so many gentlemen ogling me before."

"An enjoyable experience, to judge by your grin. I would like to think that, in this case, the gown makes the lady look like something she is not. I doubt that rake at the play would have—er—put his hand on your bottom if you had been wearing your own gown."

"That is probably true. Certainly no gentleman at home ever dared to take such a liberty. And by the way, I was not grinning! At home, they know Papa would give them a sound thrashing if they tried it. Tell me, is this bottom-patting a new fad in London? I wish to know for my next novel."

"No, it is not. What did you do when it happened?" he asked and listened with considerable interest for her reply.

"I just moved away and gave him a dirty look. I wish I had slapped him, but with so many people around, I disliked to make a fuss. That's very interesting, is it not? I didn't even give him a verbal reprimand. I allowed people's opinion to change my behavior—and character, you know, is only the sum and total of our behavior." After a frowning pause, she added, "I wonder if that is what has happened to Meg."

"It is kind of you to look for an excuse, but you're barking up the wrong tree. Meg has no aversion to having a fuss made over her. Quite the contrary."

"But to be thought provincial—that's what I really mean. I feared those people would think me a flat, and it just occurred to me that Meg is only pretending to approve of that sort of license so her new friends will like her. I thoroughly despise them in the individual, but as a group, they intimidated me. I didn't want to paint myself as being different, unaccustomed to city ways." A frown seized her brow. "Why should I care what they think?"

"When in Rome. Another of those clichés that so often prove true."

"Yes, otherwise they wouldn't be clichés. But you really ought to have encouraged me not to care what they think. I fear you're a little lax in your morals as well, Montaigne."

"I thought we had already established my debased morals by my returning Lady Dearborne's greeting at the play."

"What kind of a greeting takes ten minutes?" Before he could reply, she continued, "We learn nothing from history." She gazed solemnly into the darkness. "We know what happened to Rome, since Mr. Gibbon has outlined its decline and fall for us."

"In six volumes. Don't tell me you've read that monumental work?"

"No, I tried, but it gave me the megrims. I read the old reviews, and an essay about it in the *Tatler*. But we were speaking of Meg. Will you talk to her, Montaigne, and I shall continue working on Fairly?"

"I shall speak to Meg, but about Fairly, Sissie—you shouldn't allow yourself to become too intimate with him. He's not the sort of gentleman your papa would want you to go about with."

"How can you say so? I am a guest under his roof. That already involves a degree of intimacy."

"To be sure, but you need not go out of your way to be alone with him."

Montaigne felt a niggling tug at his conscience. He had not given this visit enough consideration. Fairly was known to pitch himself at the head of any pretty lady who gave him the time of day. Montaigne had not thought Sissie would be his type, but since Meg had smartened her up, she looked more sophisticated than she was. In fact, she looked troublesomely attractive. She had turned several heads at the Clarendon and attracted considerable attention at the play as well. Not less than three gentlemen had mentioned her. "A new Incomparable," Lord Southern had called her, and Southern was something of a connoisseur.

"He has promised to take me to visit the slums tomorrow afternoon," she said.

"I was going to take you there!" He felt annoyed, and assured himself if it had been anyone other than Fairly, any perfectly respectable gentleman, he would have been happy to be relieved of the chore.

"You didn't say so when I hinted. You said how busy you were. I can't go alone, and I must do my research. In any case, the slums are hardly a spot where he will be making up to me, if that is what you fear."

"So you do realize his intentions."

"I realize what you think. I believe he just wants a sympathetic ear to complain about Meg. I know that sort of thing can lead to romance if you let it. Mr. Edwards tried that trick with Anne at home when his wife was carrying on with Squire Higgins. Anne gave him a setdown. We had a good laugh about it. Don't worry, I shan't let Fairly get out of hand."

Her plain speaking reassured him. "Where, in the slums, are you going?"

"He mentioned some place called Seven Dials. It's in St. Giles-in-the-Fields, I believe he said. An odd name for a place. Does it actually have seven dials?" she asked, ever curious.

"It used to have seven sundials, but they've been taken away."

54

"Seven, why so many? And why were they removed?"

"I don't know." But he did know that it was a dangerous spot to take a lady. Could Fairly be counted on to protect her? "Be sure Fairly takes a few footmen with him."

The carriage reached Berkeley Square and drew to a stop in front of the Fairly residence.

"This has been a very useful evening," Cicely said, gathering up her shawl and reticule. "I should make my notes while it is all fresh in my mind, but I may wait until tomorrow morning. Would you like to come in for a cup of cocoa, Montaigne? I should love one, but I'm a little shy to ask Coddle for it. He's so supercilious."

Montaigne felt a chuckle rise up in his throat. He had forgotten Sissie's way of blurting out whatever was on her mind. What would Murray and the literary reviewers make of her?

"I am flattered at your eagerness for my company! I shall brave Coddle's wrath and demand a cup of cocoa," he replied.

While they awaited the cocoa, Montaigne noticed that Sissie kept the shawl wrapped tightly around her shoulders.

"It's a little late to be hiding your charms," he informed her. "They were on full display while you ate dinner at the Clarendon."

She laughed and let the shawl fall open. "I feel safe with you. Truth to tell, I have been uncomfortable all evening. I'm not accustomed to being half naked in public. These gowns ladies wear are asking for trouble. That is something else you might mention to Meg."

"I doubt Fairly would thank me for it," he said,

making a conscious effort to control his eyes, with only limited success.

"We shouldn't cater to the lowest taste," she said primly. When she noticed his errant eyes, she added bluntly, "I'd feel more comfortable if you could control *your* eyes, Montaigne. You must have seen hundreds of bosoms by now."

"True, but a lady's charms never fail to attract attention. I was mistaken. It is not too late to hide temptation." He reached over and tied her shawl in a knot under her chin.

When the cocoa arrived, they discussed the dinner party to be held the following evening.

"Tell me something about the reviewers who will be there. Which ones are more influential? I shall be sure to empty the butter boat on them."

"There will be a Mr. Summers, from the *Quarterly Review*. Murray started the *Quarterly* half a decade ago and has colleagues there. They'll give *Chaos* a good review. A Mr. Blackwood is starting up a new monthly periodical. The *Edinburgh Review* will be the tough nut to crack, and it's the most influential of the lot. It takes itself very seriously. They'll be sending Sir Giles Gresham. They don't plan to review *Chaos*, but if we can convince them there's a message in it, they might give us a mention."

"What do you know of Sir Giles? He's the one to go after."

"He's a scholar of classics. He'll not be flattered into submission. They're sending him only to appease Murray."

"What age is he?"

"Forty-something. A bachelor."

She gave him a coquettish smile. "A bachelor of a

certain age is always amenable to flirtation," she said, unconsciously patting the knotted shawl.

"Now, Sissie! One rake to worry about is enough. I don't want you carrying on with Sir Giles. Good God, Murray will find himself accused of trying to pervert literary reportage."

"As if his connection with the *Quarterly Review* doesn't do that! I had no notion there was so much incest in the business. But you underestimate me, milord. I shall be discreet. Only think of the poor orphans," she said, drawing a long face.

"You don't know the meaning of the word *discretion*. I begin to think it was a huge mistake to bring you here. You've only been in London half a day, and already you have Fairly trotting after you, half the ton gossiping about you, and Meg in the boughs."

"To say nothing of Lord Montaigne in an uproar and making me sit with this shawl choking me because he can't control his eyes." Montaigne could think of no answer to her charge of ogling.

"If Sir Giles is not flirtable, I shall employ flattery," she said. "Every man born of woman adores flattery."

"How will you flatter a scholar of classics without making a fool of yourself? I assume you haven't studied Latin or Greek?" He was coming to realize, however, that she had read more widely than most young girls. Where had she come across the idea of incest? She had picked up pretty quickly on the questionable ethics of Murray's association with the *Quarterly* as well.

She cast her eyes down modestly. "Indeed no. I am only a simple country girl, Lord Montaigne. We leave such scholarly pursuits to you gentlemen.

How should I hope to understand the wisdom of Socrates and Aristotle, even if I could read Latin?"

"Actually they were Greeks," Montaigne said.

Cicely gave a shy smile, allowing her long lashes to flutter a moment. "There, you see how ignorant I am. I wish I knew about such things. I want to be a really serious writer, you know. Could you recommend a good translation into English of those great philosophers for me, Montaigne?"

"I wish you would call me Monty," he said, in a warmer tone. She lifted her downcast eyes and smiled shyly at him. Montaigne began to see Cicely was really more interesting than he had imagined. There was more to her than a provincial miss. "That is very ambitious of you, my dear. I should be happy to find a copy of a good translation. I daresay I have one in my library somewhere."

"Perhaps you would lend it to me, sometime when you have a moment free, I mean. Naturally I would not impose on your important work in the House."

"I'll dig it out this very night and bring it tomorrow."

Sissie's fluttering eyelashes fell still. Her shy smile turned to an impish grin. "And you think I can't flatter an aging bachelor into submission! I have just conned *you*, Monty. You did ask me to call you Monty, did you not?"

"Good God! Hoist by my own petard."

"No, sir, by the wind of vanity."

"Not much chance for vanity when you call me an old bachelor." Was that how she saw him?

"I didn't say *old*! Don't worry. With all your blunt and an abbey besides, you're still young enough to be eligible."

"Nothing like an estate to maintain one's youthful eligibility."

"As good as Ponce de León's fountain of youth. But you underestimate your charms, Montaigne," she said, with a tinge of admiration lighting her eyes. "You have a good deal more to offer than an abbey."

"Dare I ask the meaning of that mischievous remark?"

"I refer, of course, to your title."

He glared. "Of course."

"I was just joking. You're not as bad as most of them, from what I have seen."

"Let us end the subject of my multifarious attractions on that faint praise."

"Yes, it's time for you to be leaving. My cocoa is gone. I look forward to seeing you tomorrow." Montaigne allowed a small smile to peep out. "You did promise to bring me that translation." His smile faded. Cicely's grew broader.

She rose, made a curtsy, and left. Montaigne sat on a moment, frowning at the task before him: to contain the mischief of this chit for the few days she was to remain in London.

Chapter Six

In the morning, Cicely jotted down her recollections of the previous evening while the details were fresh in her mind. That done, she began seeking out and writing up new research for her next novel. This involved not only a tour of Fairly's house but a particular perusal of Meg's room. She counted the gowns in her armoires, examined them to see what sort of ornaments were in style, and lifted the lid of each silver-topped container on her toilet table. Meg was in attendance, to explain any mysteries.

"At home, wearing rouge is considered pretty fast. Do all the young ladies wear it here?" Cicely asked.

"Three-quarters of them do. Not that they admit it. Sukey Dorman tries to pretend her color is natural, but once when she was weeping because her horrid husband wouldn't buy her a high-perch phaeton, I noticed that her handkerchief had pink smudges on it afterward."

"Why did she want a phaeton?"

"Because they are all the crack, goose!"

"Oh. And why would he not let her have one?"

"Because he had lost a thousand pounds at the card table the evening before, and naturally his wife was the one who had to pay for his sins. That is the way we are treated, Sissie. Shocking! It's not all roses, being married to a rich lord, you must know."

"Lost a thousand pounds in one evening!"

"That's nothing," Meg said. "Fairly once lost five hundred in two minutes. He and Atherly were betting on whether Lady Caroline Lamb would attend a dinner party after Byron had jilted her. She appeared at the door not two minutes later. I swear Atherly had seen her carriage draw up before he made the bet. Fairly tried to reneg on his promise to buy me a pair of cream ponies for my carriage after he lost his bet, but I made him go to the cents-per-center and borrow the money."

"How did you make him?" Cicely asked, her eyes wide.

"I made his life a living hell," Meg replied with a glinting smile at the memory. "I stayed in my room for twenty-four hours. Every time I heard him approach the door, I took a deep whiff of my hartshorn, and he found me in tears. Gentlemen can't bear to see ladies cry."

"Papa says it is folly to borrow from the usurers."

"Oh, everyone does it in London. It is the latest thing."

"Money is money in London, the same as in the country. What's borrowed must be paid—with interest. I cannot think it wise for you to encourage Fairly to borrow."

"He needs no encouragement, goose!"

"It would be horrid if he squandered all his fortune and ended up poor."

"Shocking," Meg agreed, undismayed.

"I wouldn't do as everyone else does, just to make them like me. That can easily happen in a place like London." To give her friend a foretaste of the doom awaiting her if she continued on this profligate course, Cicely asked Meg to accompany her and Fairly to the slums that afternoon.

"I've already seen them. They are very boring. Bedlam was much more amusing. Perhaps Fairly will take you there to see the lunatics tomorrow. It's kind of you to entertain him for me. It leaves me free for more interesting amusements," she said daringly.

"You aren't seeing another gentleman!" Sissie gasped.

"No, I am having my portrait painted as a surprise for Fairly." She didn't mention that the artist was an exceedingly pretty young fellow and an excellent flirt, even if he was not much of a painter.

"Then you do still love Fairly?" Sissie said, relieved to hear it.

"Of course I do, goose!" Meg said and frowned to realize she meant it. "It's just that he hasn't turned out to be the sort of husband I imagined. His first ardor faded too quickly. When new gowns and bonnets didn't quicken his love, I tried making him jealous, but he was not at all jealous of my flirts. He didn't command me to stop seeing my cicisbeo; he reciprocated by acquiring flirts of his own. If a man doesn't take charge, then he must not expect his wife to behave as he wishes." She pouted and tossed her curls. "It's nothing to get in a pelter about. It's the way everyone goes on in London. Married couples are not shackled leg and wing here. We'd be a laughingstock if we went about together."

"If I had a husband I loved I wouldn't spend so much time in London, if that's the way folks go on."

"You're a country mouse, Sissie. You will marry

some stout squire and have a nurseryful of children. To each her own."

"Fairly would like a son."

"One would never guess it by the way he behaves," Meg snipped, dipping her fingers into the rouge pot, for her mirror told her she looked like a corpse beside Sissie.

Fairly did not return for lunch. Meg waited for a quarter of an hour, and when it was clear he was not coming, she and Cicely went into the dining room without him.

"It's typical!" Meg scolded. "And I had Cook make his favorite luncheon, too. I should think that when I have company he might return, or at least tell me he would not be here. Perhaps you can find out where he was—but discreetly. I wouldn't want him to think I was prying."

"I would hardly call it prying," Cicely replied. "Surely a wife has a right to know. Papa always sends word if he's going to be even ten minutes late."

Fairly returned at three. He made a curt bow to his wife before turning a smile in Cicely's direction. "All set for our trip to the slums?" he asked. "I see you have dressed for the occasion. Very wise."

He assumed her modest gown had been chosen to avoid ostentation and lessen the risk of being robbed. The bonnet and mantle she put on were of the same provincial cut as the gown. Meg's stylish high-poke bonnet with clusters of fruit around the base of the crown rested on the banister post. He picked it up as they left the house, for he wanted to go on the strut with Cicely after they had visited Seven Dials. His reputation demanded that she appear more modish.

"Are you not bringing any footmen?" she asked when she saw only the coachman. "Montaigne thought we ought to take a couple in case we're attacked."

"I wager I can handle anything that comes along." He handed her into the carriage and arranged a fur blanket over her knees.

"Why did you bring Meg's bonnet?" she asked as the carriage lurched forward.

"Is it Meg's? I've never seen her in it. I thought it was yours. No matter. It will look dashed pretty on you later."

"I hope Meg was not planning to wear it herself."

"Going out then, is she?" he asked, with some interest. "Did she happen to mention where . . ."

"Shopping, I believe," she prevaricated. Having her portrait done *was* shopping for his birthday present. "And what marvelous things were you doing all morning, milord?"

"Demme, I wish you will call me Fairly." His morning had consisted of rounding up a pair of bruisers to accost him and Cicely at Seven Dials, to allow him to appear heroic. Naturally he couldn't tell Cicely that, but her bright eyes were looking at him expectantly.

"I had business matters to attend to," he said.

"It must be very dear to live in London," she said leadingly.

"M'dear, you don't know the half of it. Meg has spent a thousand pounds on gewgaws this month," he exaggerated, to impress her. "Three new bonnets! To say nothing of that bill from her modiste. She has ample pin money, but I am sent her bills. I should like to know how she expects me to pay for it all, on top of running the house."

"You can run into real trouble if you go to the cents-per-center. Why don't you rusticate for a few months?" she suggested.

"Ho, try to convince Meg of that! There's no one to flirt with in the country."

"Then it would leave her more time for you," she said with a playful smile.

"She is weary of my company, Sissie."

"I cannot think so, for she has very little of it, from what I have seen."

"More than she wants, I warrant."

"On the contrary. She was disappointed that you could not come home for luncheon. Meg ordered your favorite raised pigeon pie."

"She never said so!" A small smile grew on his face.

"Meg is not the type to complain."

This was news to Fairly. "And did *you* miss me, Sissie?" he asked with a conning smile, which Cicely ignored entirely.

"I enjoyed having Meg to myself. Selfish of me, but we had a great deal to get caught up on. How far away is Seven Dials?" she asked, to avoid the coming flirtation.

"Just past Charing Cross Road—not prime real estate. I'll drive you along Piccadilly first to see the real London."

The west end of Piccadilly was impressive, even in November. Green Park was still green. This idyllic spot with cattle grazing seemed out of place in the heart of London. As they turned north, the greenery and fine buildings petered out into commercial establishments, finally degenerating into hovels.

"I have never seen anything like this!" Cicely exclaimed, staring around her in disbelief when Fairly

65

announced uncertainly that he figured they were now at Seven Dials.

It made the poorhouse at home look opulent by comparison. The doors on the hovels hung crookedly, some of them on one hinge. The holes where windows had once rested were covered in oilskin or rags or brown paper. Clusters of bedraggled humanity sat on the doorsteps, huddled together for warmth, their very postures a picture of despair. What must the interior of those hovels be like, that they braved the wintry blasts to escape them? Perhaps it was the daylight that drew them, as the shacks had no glazed windows.

Some of the women had children in their arms. Most of them held a bottle of what Fairly assured her was Blue Ruin, from which they took frequent drinks. Blue Ruin shops abounded. Children roamed the streets in packs, too dispirited to play. They had the feral air of wild animals, as they slouched along, looking over their shoulders. Several fully grown men were also there.

Fairly had his ruffians waiting at the corner of Neal Street, the location chosen because of its proximity to Bow Street. He would let the lads escape, of course, but he might report them to Bow Street, to lend an air of authenticity to the attack. If, on the other hand, as he hoped, Cicely was completely overwrought, he would stay with her in the carriage, comforting her in his arms until she was sufficiently recovered to don Meg's bonnet and go for a strut on New Bond Street, where she was bound to relate his heroism to anyone they met.

"Shall we get out and have a look around?" he asked as the carriage approached Neal Street.

"I fear that would not be wise," Cicely said. "A

cutpurse would have your money before we'd gone two steps."

"I came prepared," he said, lifting a stout cudgel from the floor.

She was surprised at the dandy's willingness to involve himself in a brawl. "We might be outnumbered," she said. "I just wanted to see the place. It's worse than I imagined." Certainly her heroine's courage would be put to the test in this domestic hell.

"You need not fear, Cicely. I shall protect you," he said and pulled the drawstring, against her repeated opposition.

"No, really. This is most unwise, Fairly."

"It will provide excellent research for you, seeing how a gentleman handles these fellows," he insisted.

"But how will *they* handle a lady?"

"Ha-ha. Come along," he said, his patience wearing thin.

Cicely stuffed her reticule in the pocket of the carriage, picked up Fairly's malacca cane and got out, looking all around her. Fairly spotted his hired henchmen and began strutting toward them. The men exchanged a quiet word and began advancing.

"Come, Fairly," Cicely said, tugging at his elbow. "This is folly. I have seen how brave you are."

"There are only two of them," he said with an air of braggadocio as he quickened his pace, winking at his cohorts.

"But they're huge!"

He had paid them a pound each, in advance. They were Lord Henry Milvern's prize bruisers. Henry had assured him they would do as agreed. Fairly raised his cudgel menacingly and said, "Stand aside, lads."

"Who gave you the street, mister?" one of them answered.

The bigger of the men raised his fists and feinted a blow at Fairly's chin. Fairly dodged, lifted his cudgel, and lowered it lightly on the bruiser's shoulder. The other bruiser grabbed Fairly's left arm, yanked it behind his back, and said, "Hand over your rhino and we'll not kill you."

"Scoundrel!" Fairly said, tearing his arm free. "Desist, I say. Out of my way."

He flailed his cudgel in the air, landing the second attacker a grazing blow on the elbow. The first made another attack. Fairly fought it off with ease. A scuffle ensued. Cicely raised the cane but the ruffians jerked about so quickly she couldn't be sure of striking them without hurting Fairly.

After a short tussle, the larger man said, "All right. You can pass, but we'll keep an eye out for you another time."

Cicely was quite simply astonished that the two brutes caved in so quickly. "Let us go," she said, pulling at Fairly's coattails as he shouted brave abuse at the fleeing scoundrels.

"You have only to be firm with them," he said, his chest swelling.

As they hurried back to their waiting carriage, John Groom shouted to Fairly. "Here, milord! There's another pair of the rascals." As he spoke, he scrambled down from his perch, raising his horsewhip.

The second pair came as a dreadful surprise to Fairly. They had not been arranged for in advance. His heart quaked to see they were every bit as big

and strong as the bruisers, and with mean faces besides. Fairly had the slight advantage as one of
them was entering the carriage. He grabbed him by
his collar and swung him around. As the man
turned, his right hand rose, bunched into a fist, with
which he landed Fairly a facer. Fairly went sprawl-
ing in the dust, blood spouting from his nose. The
man made a quick lunge at his pockets.

"Help, Hawkins!" Fairly called weakly to his
groom.

The groom advanced, lashing his horsewhip. It
was not until then Cicely noticed that the other
man had gotten into the carriage and was emerging
with her reticule and Meg's bonnet in his left hand.
She lifted the malacca cane and aimed it at the side
of his head.

"Take that, villain!" she exclaimed, snatching at
her reticule. It fell open and the contents scattered
in the dust, just as Hawkins snapped his whip over
the second man's shoulder.

"Well done, mistress!" Hawkins congratulated
her.

The pair of attackers took to their heels, one of
them still holding Cicely's reticule and Meg's bonnet. She had lost her reticule, but John Groom gathered up her belongings from the street as she
tended to Fairly's bloodied nose.

"I told you we shouldn't get out of the carriage,"
she scolded. "Does it hurt very much?"

Fairly held his handkerchief to his nose, with his
head back, as Cicely and the groom herded him into
his carriage.

"It's a good thing the young lady kept her wits
about her, or you would have lost your purse,"

Hawkins said, shaking his head at Fairly's stupidity in coming here.

"Drive home at once," Cicely said.

"Bow Street is just around the corner," he advised her.

"What is the point of notifying Bow Street? Fairly will only look a fool for having got out of the carriage. No doubt there are hundreds of ruffians matching the description of those who attacked us. Just get us home."

"Aye, aye, mistress," Hawkins replied and jumped up to his perch. With another crack of his whip, they were off.

"I am terribly sorry this happened, Fairly," Cicely said. "It was really foolish of you to go on foot amid such men. But you were right about it being excellent for my research. I see now that these fellows work in pairs. One crew keeps you busy while another rifles your carriage. It's shameful that men are sunk to this sort of life. You should do something about it in Parliament."

This was not what Fairly had expected to hear, but he heard a deal more of the same as he was driven home with his aching nose ignominiously buried in his handkerchief.

"It is really not right that such poverty is allowed to exist cheek by jowl with such wealth," Cicely continued as they proceeded along Piccadilly. "Men having to rob to feed their families, while people like you enjoy a second dinner at an expensive hotel. I shall mention it to Montaigne. He is active in the House."

It was another blow to Fairly's pride that Montaigne was seen as the gentleman to do something about the situation.

"I shall certainly have a word about this with my member of Parliament," he said.

"You're a member of the House of Lords. Why do you not raise the question in the House yourself?"

"I shall, by the living jingo. It's intolerable. A man is not safe on the streets."

As they drew nigh to Berkeley Square he said sheepishly, "There is no need to mention this to Meg."

She gave him a long look. "As I shall have to borrow a reticule from her this evening, I fear I must mention it, to say nothing of her bonnet being lost. I shall be sure to tell her how you sent that first pair of bruisers running."

"Bruisers?" he exclaimed. "Why do you call them bruisers? They were not bruisers."

"I only meant great hulking brutes," she replied, surprised at his outburst.

He accepted that she was unaware that they were hired bruisers.

It was not long, however, before she began to suspect the whole. Fairly's blows had been mere taps, and those two big men had retreated with suspicious alacrity. He had arranged that first attack to make himself look brave. Was there no bottom to his vanity and stupidity? More excellent research for her novel, but Fairly was no longer a plausible hero. He would have to be only a suitor for the heroine's hand, and some other character found to carry the burden of love interest.

Chapter Seven

Cicely and Fairly reached home an hour before Meg. Cicely spent the time jotting down notes on her adventure while Fairly put himself in the hands of his valet to repair the ravages of his afternoon. They had just returned to the saloon to enjoy a restorative cup of tea when Meg landed in, fire blazing in her eyes.

"I should like to know why you took my new bonnet, Fairly," she said. "What have you done with it, eh? Given it to a light-skirt? You shall buy me two bonnets, to make up for it. You don't fool me with this excuse of showing Sissie the slums. You dumped her on your Aunt Sophronia while you went visiting one of your bits of muslin."

"Oh indeed, Meg, we were at Seven Dials," Cicely said, "and were attacked by two sets of villains. We would not have come out alive had it not been for Fairly's quick thinking and bravery in attacking them. Can you not see how red his nose is? It's been pouring blood all afternoon." She laid it on with a trowel to make Meg admire her husband.

Meg was distracted by this tale of dangerous doings. "Attacked by villains! I wish I had gone with you. What happened?"

"Two of them stole your bonnet and my reticule

72

out of the carriage while Fairly was fighting off another pair. They travel in two pairs of two."

"Shocking!" she said, turning to her husband. "And you actually tackled them, Fairly?" she asked, hardly able to credit such an unlikely tale. Yet Fairly's nose, now that Meg took a glance at it, stood out in brilliant relief against his white face.

"With a club," he said, peering soulfully at Meg.

She rushed forward to comfort him. "Oh, my poor *esposo*. Are you serving him tea, Sissie? Call for brandy. We all need a glass of brandy."

Cicely duly noted that contraband brandy was readily available in noble homes—and drunk not only by the heroes but by their wives.

"You should stay home tonight and help Fairly to recover," Cicely suggested. "He looks very peaked, does he not?"

"Stay at home?" Meg asked, and laughed. "Hardly! I shall take him to Lady Amelia's ball and show him off."

"Fairly is in no condition to dance."

"Indeed no. We shall sit out all evening. I shall wear a black shawl, to show how serious your condition is, Fairly. And you, a black sling on your arm."

To Cicely's amazement, Fairly entered into this foolishness with the greatest enthusiasm. She had no doubt that by the time they reached the ball, Fairly would be in a Bath chair and the four attackers (two of them hired, she was now convinced) would be a whole band, armed to the teeth.

"Well, you were very fortunate that Fairly was there to protect you, Sissie," Meg said. "But you have still not explained why you took my bonnet."

Cicely studied the pair and decided this was the

strategic moment to push their reformation a step further.

"Fairly was returning it to the milliner, Meg," she said, darting a commanding look at Fairly. "He realizes, if you do not, that borrowing from the cents-per-center will ruin you both. You are not to buy any more clothes this season."

Fairly looked in horrified alarm, first at Cicely, then at his wife, who—strangely—was batting her eyelashes furiously and smiling at him in a coquettish way he had not seen for a twelvemonth.

"You have enough bonnets," he said sternly. "The best turned-out lady in London. Everyone says so."

"Do you really think so, Fairly?" Meg asked, sitting down and taking his hand. She felt a warm gush of something stronger than mere pique at his high-handedness.

"Common knowledge."

Meg directed a speaking smile at him. "I must go abovestairs to change for dinner. Come with me, Fairly. I want you to help me choose what I should wear tonight."

Fairly flushed in pleasure. "You haven't asked my opinion on such things in a long time, Meg."

She turned to Cicely. "I have had my dresser put a gown for the dinner party in your room, Sissie," she said.

The couple walked upstairs together, arm in arm, whispering and smiling. Cicely was also smiling. Now if Montaigne would do his part and give Meg a good talking-to, this shambles of a marriage might yet be pulled from the fire.

She finished her tea; then, when the brandy arrived, had a sip of it for research purposes. Medicine! She left it and went abovestairs to see what she would be wearing to Mr. Murray's dinner party.

Montaigne had sent his sister a note informing her he didn't want Sissie to look like a light-skirt but a provincial lady. To Meg, this meant a gown a couple of years old, not in the empress style that currently ruled. She had scoured her closet for the most likely gown she possessed. Its provincialism was solely in its age. Neither its cut nor its lack of adornment was in the least dowdy. The gown was a dark green and silver net that shimmered under the light with the effect of water seen by moonlight. It clung closely to the body above, flaring out in a full skirt below. Once again a shawl was required to conceal the paucity of material from the waist up, but the shawl had to be arranged with care to display Anne's diamonds. As Meg had not provided a shawl, Cicely used Anne's white wool.

The Fairlys were having guests to dinner that evening. Before they arrived, Lord Montaigne came to escort Cicely to Murray's party. His eyes turned to her at once to judge her toilette. His somewhat strained expression softened to pleasure as he studied her.

With her shawl firmly wrapped around her shoulders, she looked modest. Her dark gown was a matronly shade, and that white shawl had a whiff of the country in its sturdy material. The coiffure was pretty, without reaching such heights of elegance that it competed with Meg's do.

"You will never guess what, Monty!" Meg exclaimed. "Fairly is a hero! I am going to Lady Amelia's ball with him this evening." She studied her brother eagerly for his reply to such shocking news.

75

"I hardly know which piece of news is more startling," he said in a bored drawl. He suspected that Sissie was involved in both events. He looked a question at her. Her laughing eyes belied her innocent expression. "What heroic deed has he done? Not a duel in your honor, I trust, Meg? That is a shade too heroic for Society. Duels are out of fashion this year."

"No, silly. He beat up a whole gang of armed bandits who attacked him and Sissie at that horrid place with all the dials. Was there ever anything so shocking! They got away with my new bonnet," she added with a moue.

Montaigne turned in alarm to Sissie. He was reassured to see she was not only unharmed but having some difficulty controlling her amusement.

Before Montaigne could learn the real story, Fairly came limping in with his arm in a sling to help his nose recover. He at once delivered a much-embroidered version of the attack. As Sissie had anticipated, the four men had grown to an indeterminate number, but certainly more than four.

"Fairly is going to raise the subject in the House," Meg said proudly when the tale was told.

"Is he, by God?" Montaigne exclaimed. "I shall show you where your seat is, Fairly," he added with a touch of cynicism.

"And you must show me where the visitors' gallery is," his sister said. "I shall take a group to hear him. Do they serve wine as they do at the theater at intermission, or must we take our own?"

"I should hold the wine until you reach home, Meg," he replied. "No doubt you will be having a party to celebrate Fairly's maiden speech in the House."

"What a gorgeous idea! A speech party! Why did I not think of it? It is so difficult to find new excuses for an afternoon party. I shall invite the prime minister."

Montaigne drew a deep sigh. "I doubt a Tory prime minister will be interested. An occasion of this sort is strictly partisan." Meg frowned in confusion. "Your husband is a Whig," he informed her.

"Oh, yes, of course. I must warn the ladies not to wear anything blue. True blue and Tory, too—is that not what folks say? Pity, when I look so well in blue."

"P'raps you would give me a hand with my speech, Monty," Fairly said. "Sissie thinks I should mention poverty. What do you think?"

"That would dilute the aroma of self-interest," Monty agreed with a nod of appreciation at Sissie.

When Montaigne had escorted Sissie out, he turned a quizzing look on her. "What really happened this afternoon?" he asked and assisted her into his carriage.

She always felt like a princess when she stepped into Montaigne's beautiful crested chaise. She felt a pang for the denizens of Seven Dials as he placed the fur rug over her knees.

"I believe Fairly hired a pair of bruisers to hold us up, so he could act the hero. Unfortunately—or fortunately, as it turned out—two real ones got into the carriage during the performance and stole my reticule and Meg's bonnet. Fairly got his nose punched during the fracas. I succeeded in convincing Meg he is a hero."

"I assume Hawkins handled the fellows? You weren't hurt?"

"No, I wasn't. Fairly had taken along a cudgel, so

I used his walking stick. Hawkins and I managed to subdue the real thieves."

In the darkness of the carriage, Montaigne allowed a smile to peep out. It came as no surprise that Sissie had rescued herself. He was coming to realize she was a lady of many accomplishments.

"I'm surprised you let the fellows snatch Meg's bonnet from your head."

"I wasn't wearing it. Fairly brought it for me to wear when we went on the strut later. I hope Fairly carries through on his promise to raise the matter in the House. It was incredible, Montaigne. The poverty, the real destitution. Is there nothing that can be done about it?"

"The Whigs are taking an interest in the matter. Such major changes are needed that it will take time. Education and jobs are the crux of the matter. Private charities don't go far, as I am learning."

"The earnings from *Chaos*—"

"An orphanage, for some of the worst cases," he said curtly. "I suggested it to my aunt."

"I feel a wretch for teasing you about the orphans. I had no idea until I had seen them myself. You have been to Seven Dials, I think?"

"Yes, I have been there and other places. But we shan't discuss all that now and spoil your party."

"It doesn't spoil it," she said in a pensive tone. "It just makes me realize how important it is. I shall give some of my earnings to charity as well—if I sell my novel, I mean."

To lighten the mood, Montaigne inquired how Cicely had liked Bond Street.

"As things turned out, we didn't get there after all. That is one thing I should like to do before I leave London. It might be best if you could accompany me. I would not like to put Meg in temptation's path. Fairly has forbidden her to buy anything else this Season."

Montaigne's head turned slowly to gaze through the shadows to his partner. "I beg your pardon?"

"The little altercation with the thieves painted Fairly as a temporary hero. When Meg inquired why her bonnet was in the carriage, I told her Fairly was returning it to the milliner because she was spending too much money. A plumper, of course, but for a good cause."

"And she swallowed that?"

"She was thrilled to death at his daring."

"I find that hard to believe. Meg without a new bonnet is like—like Prinny without a new jacket."

"Oh Monty, don't you know *anything* about ladies? They make a fuss about being independent, but they really like to think their husband is a strong man, one who takes charge and looks after their best interest. They went upstairs together almost immediately. Meg was making big eyes at him. I'm sure they were going to—" She stopped.

"Yes, you were saying?" he asked, enjoying a silent laugh at her predicament.

"You know what I mean. I see that as an excellent sign," she said, trying for an air of dignity. "I only hope something comes of it. I'm convinced a child would do them both a world of good. They couldn't act like children themselves if they had a real child to worry about. I have done my bit; it remains only for you to read Meg a lecture, and I believe the marriage may be saved yet."

Montaigne considered the notion of chiding Cicely for intimating what might have gone forth between Meg and Fairly in their bedchamber, but he let it pass. It would only lead her on to some worse solecism.

"It wouldn't have come to a divorce," he said.

"They would probably have gone on inhabiting the same house for the looks of it. That's not my idea of marriage. A marriage means sharing all of life, its hardships and victories."

"Till death do us part, in fact. It's that suggestion of a life sentence that puts me off the notion of marriage."

"Me, too," she said, surprising him. "I have never yet met a gentleman with whom I could envisage sharing the rest of my life, but those who have made the bargain ought to live up to it. Marriage is a gamble, in a way, and a gentleman, I understand, always pays his gambling debts. His debt, in this case, is to his wife. And I am not talking about money."

"A very pretty piece of sophistry, Miss Cicely. Where is the gamble when one is guaranteed losing his freedom for the temporary pleasure of enjoying a pretty lady's company? Talk about loaded dice! That is not a gamble, it is a life sentence."

She scowled at him in the darkness. "What about children? A man needs a son and heir. One would never guess you cared for children, the way you talk. What about those orphans you spoke of, that the Whigs are trying to help?"

"That is a different matter entirely. One cannot blame the children. They are helpless victims. I help them to assuage my conscience." As Cicely didn't reply, Montaigne peered at her through the darkness and spied a smile. "Why are you laughing at me?"

"I never heard a man making excuses for his generosity before."

"Don't go turning me into a saint, Sissie. I would not want to see myself canonized in your next opus."

"How did you know I was on the lookout for a hero? Fairly failed me entirely. Perhaps I shall find someone tonight at the party."

With a thought of the guests, Montaigne replied, "I shouldn't think so."

The dinner party was held at the Pulteney Hotel. As it was in honor of a lady, Murray had included the wives of his guests in the invitation. Murray was a youngish gentleman to have attained such prominence in the field of literature. He was not yet in his forties. He introduced Cicely to his wife, who expressed admiration for *Chaos Is Come Again*, then presented Cicely to the one literary giant he had managed to bring to his table, George Crabbe.

This aging widower was a modest gentleman who was vicar at Trowbridge, in Wiltshire. Cicely fell speechless when she was introduced to this legend.

"Oh, Mr. Crabbe, I have read *The Village* dozens of times," she said, shaking his hand firmly. "My copy is literally falling apart. I wish I had it with me for you to autograph. Anne would never believe it! Anne is my sister."

"You have good taste, Miss Cicely," Murray said, smiling to see his new writer was happy with only one luminary to honor her. "Everyone from Dr. Johnson to Lord Byron counts Mr. Crabbe among their favorite poets. You will be happy to hear I'm bringing out a new edition of Crabbe's works, along with a new piece he is working on."

"What is it called? I shall be on the lookout for it," Cicely said eagerly.

"It is called *Tales of the Hall*," Crabbe said, smiling almost shyly at such praise. "I'm afraid I cannot say I have read your novel, Miss Cicely, but my housekeeper has been late with my tea the past week. I cannot get her nose out of your book."

"You wouldn't like it," Cicely said. "It's a gaudy thing. You write about real life. That is what I should like to do."

Murray and Montaigne exchanged a startled glance. "There is room for everything under the broad mantle of literature," Murray said. "Some prefer Byron, some Mrs. Radcliffe, and—"

"And those with good taste prefer Mr. Crabbe," Cicely said.

Murray hustled her away, with Montaigne on her other side. "When you meet Sir Giles Gresham, it might be best to not insult your own book," Montaigne said rather testily.

"You said I must be particularly nice to Sir Giles, as Mr. Murray doesn't own his magazine. Which one is Sir Giles?"

"I wouldn't say I own the *Quarterly Review*," Murray objected. "I have an interest in it. They have their own editors and editorial policies."

Cicely gave him a cagey smile. "The one who pays the piper calls the tune, *n'est-ce pas*? I am sorry, Mr. Murray. I didn't realize it was a secret that you exert an influence beyond your book-publishing firm. How very convenient for your authors."

She was led to a tall, ascetic-looking gentleman who stood by himself in one corner, his lips curled in distaste as he stared at the assembled guests through a quizzing glass. His chestnut hair had silver wings, giving him an air of distinction.

"Sir Giles, I would like to present my new writer, Miss Cicely Caldwell," Murray said. "How did you like that copy of *Chaos* I sent you?"

"Well-named, Mr. Murray," Sir Giles said in a drawling voice. "I've not laid eyes on such a chaotic load of mumbo jumbo since your Byron landed on the scene to pervert public taste."

"He has certainly tapped into something the public craves."

"Yes, sensationalism. Bread and circuses, sir. Lord Byron provides the circus."

"*Childe Harold* is still selling remarkably well."

"There will always be a market for pornography, unfortunately. I see his *English Bards and Scotch Reviewers* gathering dust at the bookstalls. A spiteful, childish rant." He lifted his quizzing glass and stared at Cicely. "So this is your new star. She is younger than I thought."

Cicely smiled demurely. "Young enough to improve the quality of my writing, I hope, Sir Giles. I do appreciate your kindness in giving a sincere critique. Most gentlemen, you must know, only give the false coin of flattery. I hope we have time for a long chat this evening, and you can tell me all the things in my horrid book that require improving in my next effort."

Sir Giles stared at her a moment, suspecting irony. Cicely stared back demurely at the enlarged eye behind the quizzing glass. Sir Giles's sneer softened to condescension.

"I daresay I could give you a few pointers," he said.

Murray darted off to rearrange the seating. Sir Giles was to have the seat at Miss Cicely's right hand. Cicely gave Montaigne a conning smile that did nothing to reassure him of her ability to carry off her plan.

"Well, Monty, how am I doing so far?" she asked in a low voice as he led her to the table.

"Sir Giles didn't come down in the last rain. He won't be so easy to con as you think."

"But he is a bachelor," she said. She then unfolded her shawl, which added considerably to Montaigne's sense of foreboding. He saw that the modest-seeming gown was extremely revealing. Gresham might be an old stick who railed against pornography, but if he had any blood at all in his veins, he would be inflamed by those tantalizing, creamy globes.

When Montaigne realized where his thoughts were wandering, he pulled himself back to attention and scowled.

"I have always regretted being so full-figured," Sissie said. "A thin figure is so much more elegant, but I see these ridiculous appendages have some use after all."

"Cover yourself up!" he said sharply.

"If Lady Godiva could reveal her legs to free her people from servitude, then I can reveal my breasts to help the orphans."

"Let us hope Gresham realizes the role you are playing—and remembers Peeping Tom was blinded for his impertinence."

"If they blinded a man for ogling, there would scarcely be a man in London who has the use of his eyes."

Lord Montaigne's response was inaudible, but it sounded remarkably like the growling of a cur.

Chapter Eight

Montaigne, who had originally been assigned the seat next to Cicely, was now placed across the table from her. He could overhear only snatches of her conversation with Sir Giles. What he heard annoyed him to no small degree. Cicely was casting herself at Giles's feet like an apostle seeking guidance from the Lord. It did not improve Montaigne's temper to hear Sir Giles eviscerating his novel, and Sissie agreeing with every word.

"The ending was totally unrealistic," Sir Giles scoffed. "That marriage to Lord Ravencroft and the hint at nothing but bliss to come. Any novel that ends in marriage is a tragedy waiting to occur. You young romantics ought to be required by law to write a sequel. Then we should see how far those buckets of tears get your heriones. Any sane man would wring the wench's neck—if he survived drowning in her ocean of tears."

"It was only a novel," was her sole defense, since she agreed with him heartily. But did she have to say it so apologetically?

"I see you are going by Dr. Johnson's definition: A small tale, generally of love. We may assume that was one of the doctor's little jokes. My definition would be a prose work of fiction with realistic characters enacting a realistic plot. Anything else is a fairy tale."

"I couldn't agree with you more, Sir Giles. My first novel is a young girl's romantic ramblings. What novels do you think I should read to improve my skills?" This was not mere flattery. Cicely did agree with Sir Giles and was eager to harvest the gleanings of a well-read mind.

"Burney, of course. Edgeworth."

"Would you include Walter Scott? He is so popular."

"Scott ought to be hanged. He has done the novel more harm with his Highland tales than Byron has done to poetry. When a piece of writing is universally popular, you may rest assured it is tripe," Sir Giles said categorically. "Scott has a facility for words—as you have yourself, Miss Cicely."

"Thank you," she said with a tight little smile. Sir Giles had just made one speech to displease her. She wanted her book to be good, but she also wanted it to be monstrously popular.

"Credit where credit is due. You are young. When you outgrow the fantastical notions of girlhood, I have no doubt you will write something worth reading. I shall add, as a suggestion, that you not devote such labored paragraphs to your heroine's eyes in your next effort."

This elicited a girlish giggle. "And violet eyes at that!"

"Also lavender, purple, gentian and if I am not mistaken, amethyst," Sir Giles said severely. "This straining after novelty is another thing to be on your guard against. When you must distinguish your characters with such salient physical characteristics, it is fourpence to a groat the real character is wanting. Those violet eyes did your Eugenie a disservice."

Sir Giles was finding Miss Cicely entirely conversable. It was refreshing to discover a successful novelist who did not believe herself above criticism.

"I wonder she did not compare them to grape jam, as they were every other shade of purple," Cicely said, laughing.

Montaigne overheard this and gave a jump of alarm. *"She!"* It was as good as announcing Cicely had not written the demmed book herself.

Sir Giles interpreted her faux pas in a quite different manner. "That will not do, Miss Cicely, calling yourself 'she,' in an effort to disclaim Eugenie as a creature of your own imagination. Come now, confess Eugenie was based on your idealized version of yourself."

"Indeed she was not! Eugenie was everything I am not. I based her on—a lady I know, at home in Kent," she invented.

"I made sure you were going to say the tale was based on Miss Davis. Because of those violet eyes, you know."

"Miss Davis? I never heard of her. Who is she?"

Montaigne's hands clenched into white-knuckled fists upon hearing the name. Sir Giles spoke in a low voice, but during a lull in the table talk, Montaigne overheard enough to fear his secret was out.

"Why, as you are a friend of Montaigne's, I assumed you knew her. She and Montaigne were very close last spring. Everyone expected it would come to a match, but in the end a duke offered for her, and she went for the greater title." He inclined his head closer and said in a low voice, *"Entre nous,* if Lady Fairly had ever learned the alphabet, I would have suspected her of penning *Chaos*, for she was a bosom bow of Miss Davis. But of course the lady is illiterate, and in any case, we now know the author."

Cicely looked across the table. She met Montaigne's thundercloud of a frown staring back at her. She gave him a saucy grin, then turned to Sir Giles and said, in no low voice, "And was Lord Montaigne quite heartbroken at her refusal?"

"Ankle-broken, actually, unless that was an excuse to hide from Society until whatever was broken had mended. The *on dit* was that he busted his ankle in a tumble from his nag and was sent to bed a month to recuperate."

"How very sad. Why, it is enough to turn a gentleman against marriage." She looked at Montaigne. He was glaring balefully at her now. She raised her glass in a toast to him, then said to Sir Giles, "Do tell me all about Miss Davis. Does she really have violet eyes?"

"Indeed she has. They may soon be watering as copiously as Eugenie's, for one hears of trouble with the ducal match."

"It sounds quite as romantical as *Chaos*, does it not?"

"You omitted the realistic part, however—the postmarriage part."

"I begin to suspect you are a confirmed misogamist, sir, and therefore a poor judge of any novel that provides a lady a happy ending."

"Marriage is a necessary institution. A happy marriage is possible, between the right couple. I do not refer to a Darby and Joan couple, gazing contentedly into the grate while they sup their posset,

88

talking of cows and pigs, but to a civilized, urban lady and gentleman of like tastes and like fortunes."

It occurred to Sir Giles that Miss Cicely fulfilled some small part of his requirements. She was civilized, and young enough to have her taste improved. What he did not know was the extent of her fortune, but at the rate *Chaos* was selling, it would soon be greater than his own, which was not very great.

"Where will you find a lady whose taste reaches the rarefied heights of your own, Sir Giles?" she asked with a teasing smile.

"I make no claim to intellectual heights. If others say so, then it speaks of their own lack. I merely prefer good books to bad. A book like *Chaos* fulfills a purpose, a sort of opium for the lower class, who enjoy a love story. It is not a great book, but it is good in its way. Light entertainment."

"Then you will not castigate me in your magazine? It is to your review that one looks for a *real* critique."

"I cannot promise a puffing piece, but I do understand this is your first effort. We gentlemen are always sympathetic to young maidens. My publication does not usually review romantic novels, but perhaps an essay on that *sort* of writing for the masses, with *Chaos* used as an example. A good example. I do not think you will dislike what I have to say."

"You are too kind, Sir Giles," Cicely simpered.

They continued their conversation throughout the meal. Before it was over, Sir Giles condescended to say he would enjoy another opportunity to discuss her next work with her. Cicely expressed all the delight he expected, and said shyly that she had something written already. Despite his heavy burden of work, he agreed to look at it. When he asked if he might have the pleasure of driving out with her the next morning, she was in alt.

The Murrays had not planned any formal entertainment after dinner. George Crabbe agreed to give a reading from his new work. The party broke up early. Cicely felt she had some reason to crow, after her success with Sir Giles. Montaigne, however, was in the boughs as he drove her to Berkeley Square.

"There was no need to grovel to the jackanapes," he scowled.

"I thought he was charming. I agreed with nearly everything he said—including Miss Davis's violet eyes. Oh, pardon me. That is, Eugenie's violet eyes. Who really wrote the book, Montaigne? Was it Miss Davis? Did you get me to come as a favor to your lost love?"

"Don't be ridiculous. Aunt Irma wrote it."

"Surely you mean Aunt Ethel!"

He stiffened in alarm. "That's what I meant, Aunt Ethel. And she doesn't even know Debora, so obviously any resemblance is a coincidence."

"Were you very much in love with her?"

"I thought so at the time," he admitted.

"That, of course, was before you turned against marriage. She would have done better to marry you. Sir Giles said she and her duke are not getting along. *I* think she wrote the book when she realized her mistake, giving it the happy ending that escaped her in real life."

"Sir Giles is misinformed," he said firmly. "Debora and the duke are well matched. He gives her whatever she asks for."

"Like Meg and Fairly, you mean?"

90

"Like Meg and Fairly and most happily married couples."

"I am surprised you allow there is any such thing. We shall agree to disagree on what constitutes a happy marriage. Sir Giles feels as I do, that a happy marriage requires two like-minded, rational people."

Montaigne felt a spurt of annoyance. "Rational people don't get married!" he said, venting his wrath.

"I expect it is the exception when two rational people have the felicity to meet and fall in love. When that happens, surely their good sense compels them to marry. Sir Giles was saying—"

"You have been discussing marriage with Sir Giles already, have you? One of you is a fast worker. Since Sir Giles is pushing fifty, one can hardly accuse him of undue haste. That leaves yourself, Sissie." He gave her a scalding look, which she ignored. "Found your new hero, have you? An aging self-styled critic?"

"We discussed marriage in the abstract, as an idea, not in specifics. It is odd, though; Anne said I might meet a potential husband here. And incidentally, Sir Giles is closer to forty than fifty. He is forty-two."

"Do you feel you have met your potential husband in this rational gentleman more than twice your age?"

"Every unattached gentleman a lady meets is a potential husband."

"It was only a few hours ago you voiced your reluctance to marry."

"So I did, but reluctance can always be talked away by the right man. We ladies are optimists who invariably feel we can make a silk purse from whatever sow's ear turns up, as the alternative is to be a spinster, shunted from pillar to post. His age doesn't bother me. I admire his mind. We shall see how our visit goes tomorrow."

"I was to take you to Bond Street tomorrow," Montaigne reminded her with another of those sharp jabs of annoyance.

"Sir Giles is coming in the morning. He wants to discuss *Chaos Is Come Again* in more detail, for the pièce he is writing for the *Edinburgh Review*."

This good news jerked Montaigne out of his pique. "He is doing a whole piece?"

"Yes, a sympathetic piece."

"Then I daresay you must keep him in curl until it is done," he said reluctantly.

"For the sake of the orphans," she added, not with her usual mischievous grin, but with real concern. "That is not the only reason I am going out with him, however. He is just the mentor I require for my writing. I hope to lure him into a correspondence after I return to Elmdale."

"Charming. It hasn't taken London long to debauch you."

"*Honi soit qui mal y pense.* Naturally I don't mean a clandestine exchange of billet-doux but a professional correspondence. He will suggest books for me to read, and so on. Perhaps he has a translation of the classical scholars to lend me, as a certain someone failed to bring me the copy he *promised*."

"I looked! I don't happen to have it in my London house. I expect it is in the library at the abbey."

"Never mind. Sir Giles will tell me where I can buy a copy for myself. I want his opinion of the book

92

I have already written, too. I think he will like it better than *Chaos*."

"I agreed to show Murray your book. That was our bargain."

"I should appreciate Sir Giles's opinion as well."

As it was still early when they returned to Berkeley Square, Montaigne invited himself in for a glass of wine. He did not remain long, however. He had heard quite enough of the wonders of Sir Giles Gresham for one evening. And to cap his disgust, the mawworm had told Sissie about Debora Davis. With Sissie's sharp intuition, she would soon leap to the truth—that he had written *Chaos Is Come Again* himself.

But after he drove home, it was not about Sir Giles's revealing his secret that he worried. It was that Sissie would soon be imagining she was in love with the mawworm. She was still a green girl, even if Meg had rigged her out to look like a dasher. Sir Giles might think she was older and more worldly than she was—and certainly richer, after reaping the rewards of *Chaos*.

Montaigne had brought Sissie to London; she was under his protection. There was no counting on the chit to behave herself. He could hardly send her dashing back to Elmdale tomorrow, but the next morning, bright and early, he would send her home.

Yet this did not entirely please him, either. It seemed rude, surly. She had done him a great service. He ought to reward her in some manner. Take her to a rout party. The Fairlys were giving her rack and manger. Fairly had replaced him in one outing; Sir Giles was visiting her. It would be too shabby for him not to entertain her a little, after asking her to come here. She would enjoy a fashionable rout party, for her research.

He mentally scanned the invitations he had received, and chose Lady Radcliffe's rout for the next evening. Meg would lend her a gown. He began imagining Sissie in various gowns he had seen on Meg. Really very dashing gowns. No wonder the gents were all falling over her. He would ask her to wear her own gown with the new ribbons. A fond smile curved his lips, to think of Sissie romping about in her provincial gown, no doubt with a surfeit of bows. She would still be the prettiest girl there. When had Sissie Caldwell blossomed into a beauty? Even Murray had been warm in his praise of her looks.

"She could set the ton on its ear," he had said. "Byron's handsome phiz does his sales no harm, you must know, Monty. Only see how she is prying the smiles out of that mummy, Gresham."

It was an intriguing notion, not only for the increased sales, but for some research of his own. The Christmas recess would soon begin at the House. He would have time free to write. He had written one novel about a watering pot. Murray wanted another book. Cicely would be a completely different sort of heroine: a country girl, green as grass, but bossy, opinionated, interfering, intelligent, managing. No, no one would ever buy it ... would they? Of one thing he was certain: he would not make Sir Giles its hero.

Chapter Nine

Montaigne was well aware that a lady required advance notice to prepare herself for a party. He planned to invite Sissie to Lady Radcliffe's rout when he took her to Bond Street that afternoon. By ten, he felt a nagging concern that he was leaving it too late. Gresham was seeing her at eleven. The wretch would probably invite her to some dull literary lecture in the evening. He dashed off a note as he sat in the House, and handed it to one of the pages to deliver to Berkeley Square at once.

He was on edge all that morning, without quite knowing why. Gresham was a bumptious bore, but he was not a lecher after all. At the midmorning break, the party whip drew Montaigne aside and said, "Whatever is ailing you, I suggest you attend to it, then return to the House and perform your duties properly. Brougham expected you to speak against Eldon's bill. You left him with only Danville to refute those ridiculous statistics."

Such an impertinence would normally have received a sharp rebuke from Montaigne, but on this occasion, he knew he was at fault. "It was only the first reading. I shall deliver my attack in good time," he replied.

He took the whip's advice and left early to visit

Berkeley Square. Sissie had not yet returned from her outing, but Meg and Fairly were at home, sitting on the sofa, holding hands. This display of conjugal affection was not entirely a new thing. The Fairly marriage was one of extremes; they tended to swing from billing and cooing to shouting and throwing the crockery at each other.

"You are the first person we have allowed in to see us all morning," Meg announced. "We have had to turn a dozen callers from the door, because of Fairly's condition."

"Not coming down with the flu, I hope?" Montaigne inquired.

"Ninnyhammer," Meg said. "It is his sprained elbow, from fighting off that vicious band of brigands yesterday at Seven Dials."

"I thought it was his nose."

"That, too. Have you prepared his speech for the House?"

"I didn't agree to write it!" Montaigne said testily. "Merely to give some advice."

The idea of Fairly's actually wasting an afternoon in Parliament was beginning to lose its luster. Meg said, "You should have seen us at Lady Amelia's rout last night, Monty. The whole world was attending on us. I swear the hostess could scarcely make up two sets for the cotillion. Mr. Weber thinks it ought to be written up as a play. We are trying to decide whether to attend Covent Garden this evening, or Lady Radcliffe's rout."

"If Fairly cannot dance, then surely the play—"

"But could anyone see the sling when we are just sitting in a box? Of course he would rest his arm on the ledge, but it is rather dark."

"Ah, then in that case, the rout would be better medicine. I plan to take Sissie to Radcliffe's."

"She didn't say so," Meg said.

"Did she not get my note before she left?" he asked. Meg didn't know. "I plan to ask her, at any rate. That's why I am here."

He poured himself a glass of wine and tried to make sensible conversation with the Fairlys. The quarter of an hour until Sissie's return seemed endless. He felt that a morning of Gresham's prosing pomposity might be enough to show Sissie the man was a consummate bore. But when she finally arrived, her eyes were shining. Her whole face seemed lit up from within.

"You will never guess what!" she exclaimed, even before saying good day. For one absurd moment, Montaigne felt she had had an offer. "I am going to write a skit for the Christmas pantomime at Covent Garden!" she continued. "Did you ever hear of anything so marvelous? Sir Giles introduced me to a Mr. Palin, who is in charge of it. He—Mr. Palin—was lamenting the lack of some light entr'acte filler, and Sir Giles said that I had a light touch and a great facility for words."

"I thought a pantomime didn't have words," Fairly said.

"It didn't used to have, but it's grown into a sort of fairy tale, with singing and dancing and jokes," Cicely explained. "The role of the principal boy is always played by a woman, and the dame by a man, to add to the humor, you see."

"By Jove, that sounds good! I do like a masquerade." Fairly smiled.

"How will you write it in time for Christmas?"

Montaigne demanded. "The actors will have to rehearse."

"It's only a short skit," Sissie told him. "I can write it in a day or two. I have dozens of ideas."

Montaigne felt that as it was *Chaos* that had given Sissie the credentials for the job, it should be himself who wrote it, but with Fairly in the room, he couldn't say so. He attacked on a different front.

"You'll send the work from Elmdale, will you? That might be awkward. They're bound to want changes. They always do."

"Silly!" Meg said. "She will stay here."

Cicely looked her gratitude. "Would I be a terrible nuisance, Meg? I could ask Anne to come. We would put up at a cheap hotel. It would only be for a few days. I daresay Anne would enjoy it."

"What of your papa?" Montaigne asked, though he felt a twinge of pity at that "cheap hotel." "Anne never likes to leave him alone."

"It's not as though he were ill. For a special occasion like this, he wouldn't mind."

"Rubbish! You're staying here," Fairly insisted.

Montaigne felt a deep-seated aversion to the scheme. Russel Palin was a well-known womanizer. He felt in his bones it was Sissie's looks, not her (or his own) talent that had won her the commission. How could he look after her if she was hobnobbing about Covent Garden with rakes and actors?

"What had Gresham to say about it?" he asked, sensing that that pretentious bore would despise the scheme.

"He was delighted for me. Oh, and he has agreed to read *Georgiana*. I gave him my copy." The Fairlys looked at her in confusion. "That is the title of my book. I told you about it, Montaigne."

"I thought it was called *Chaos Is Here*," Fairly said, frowning.

"No, no, not that horrid thing," Sissie said. "It is another book I have written."

"Another? By Jove, you are a caution, Sissie. Dashed off another already, eh? And a pantomime as well. Grind 'em out like sausages. Sit down and tell us all about it. We are bored to flinders."

Meg sensed her *esposo* was becoming irritable with the lack of company and took her decision. "You must have a good lie-down to prepare for the rout this evening, Fairly. I shall ask Coddle to bring us up a bottle of wine."

"Then it is to be the rout?" he asked, brightening.

"No one would see us at the theater. You must tell me what gown to wear." She rose and tenderly assisted her husband to his feet. With Meg's arm around his waist, he hobbled off.

Montaigne poured Cicely a glass of wine. When he handed it to her, he sat beside her. "So Gresham has condescended to have a look at your book, eh?"

"Not just to read it, but to analyze it and tell me how to improve it. It is very kind of him, for he is excessively busy with his work on the *Edinburgh Review*."

Montaigne gritted his teeth and continued civilly. "How did you enjoy your drive through the fleshpots of London? I trust Gresham didn't steal my thunder and take you to visit the shops?"

A small frown creased her brow. "We didn't even drive by the fleshpots. Sir Giles had to pick up some books at Hatchard's. We spent the morning there, where we met Mr. Palin. It was excessively interesting. Sir Giles has recommended dozens of books I ought to read. I have written them down."

"With a translation of the classics into English heading the list. Then you will be writing your papa to tell him you have been invited to stay a little longer. It has occurred to me that you should attend a few fashionable parties as well—for your research."

Her eyes glowed with pleasure. "I should like it of all things. I feared that with Fairly malingering I would hardly get my nose out the door, but it seems they are attending a rout this evening. Do you think they mean to take me along?"

"I doubt it has so much as crossed their collective minds that they have a guest in the house. I wrote you a note asking you to go to Lady Radcliffe's rout this evening with me."

A look of pleasure and surprise beamed out. "Really? I must have left before it came. Thank you, Montaigne. I should love to go. I shall feel guilty, knowing Sir Giles is spending his evening reading my novel while I dance the night away."

"I hoped he would be writing his review of *Chaos*," Montaigne said, his lips thinning in annoyance at her harping on Gresham.

"He has already done that. He speaks well of the book. He has given me a rough copy. Would you like to see it?" She drew a crumpled page from her reticule and handed it to him.

He took it eagerly. As his eyes scanned the page, his first smile dwindled to dissatisfaction. Such condescending phrases as "a more than acceptable effort from a young girl" and "a facility for phrasing that saves a trite plot from ennui" were hardly flattering.

"I wonder what you would consider a bad review," he said when he had finished.

"Considering the nature of the novel, it is not at all bad. He takes only one stab at the violet eyes, you see. 'A little unnecessary reliance on physical appearance.' I am sure his attack would have been more venomous if I had not turned him up sweet."

Again Montaigne felt that burning sensation in his chest. "May one ask how you accomplished that—in plain daylight, in Hatchard's bookshop? Dumped the butter boat on him, eh?"

"The review was written last night, actually." She gave Montaigne a saucy look and added, "If I had had another visit to work on him, no doubt he would have proclaimed the book a marvel."

"You sound remarkably confident of your charms."

"And you, sir, sound remarkably peevish, considering that I am doing you a favor, not vice versa. You didn't even congratulate me on getting the assignment to write the pantomime but only started hinting in that odious way that I was overstaying my welcome."

Montaigne realized he was in the wrong and felt churlish for his behavior. "If I forgot to congratulate you, I am sorry."

"You did. I thought you would be happy for me. Sir Giles was thrilled to death. He thinks that with work and guidance, I could be the next Frances Burney," she said, smiling shyly.

It was that smile that goaded Montaigne into an angry outburst. "The guiding hand is to be Sir Giles's, I daresay? Mind he doesn't guide you into oblivion. He has been trying to peddle his own novel for two years. A great, thundering bore of a book. No doubt that is why he went to that do last night, to ingratiate Murray."

"How can you be so horrid, Montaigne?" she

charged. Unshed tears sprang to her eyes. Embarrassed, she brushed them away with the back of her hand, like a child. "He has been excessively kind to me. What chance would I ever have had to write for Covent Garden were it not for his introducing me to Mr. Palin?"

"I wager it was your *beaux yeux* that got you the commission, not Gresham's clout. Your looks and my book—the book I asked you to pose as the author of," he added hastily. Sissie was upset and didn't notice the slip.

"I daresay *Chaos* had something to do with it," she allowed. "In fact, Mr. Palin said as much, but I know I can do it. It will be good advertising for my own book, when it comes out. *If* it comes out, I mean. If Sir Giles likes it."

"It is not Sir Giles you have to please! I told Murray I'd send him the book today. When is Gresham to return it?"

"When he finishes reading it. He's very busy."

"Busy poking his nose in where it isn't wanted. And on top of it all, you're *using* him."

"You were happy enough when I used him to give *Chaos* a good review! Why shouldn't I use his influence to help myself as well as your Aunt Ethel? And I'm not using him. We are friends. Friends are happy to help each other—as I am helping you by being here."

Montaigne opened his mouth to continue arguing but could suddenly find nothing to say. He had encouraged her to make use of Gresham to puff off *Chaos*. Sissie was doing him a favor, and she was a friend. He should be happy for her. Why did he feel this aching worry to think of her working for Palin?

"Palin is a notorious womanizer," he said. "You want to watch yourself with him."

She looked at him with a question in her eyes. "Is that what's worrying you, Montaigne? As if he'd bother with me when he is surrounded by beautiful actresses all day. I shan't be seeing much of Palin, in any case. He's one of the managers, but he only chooses the author. It is the director I will be working with. A Mr. Moore, who, Sir Giles tells me, is an elderly gentleman."

"If Gresham called him elderly, he must be ancient. Just keep your distance from Palin," he said.

She glared but refused to rise to the bait. "Are you staying for lunch?" she asked.

"No, I just dropped in early to let you know about Lady Radcliffe's rout party. I didn't want Gresham to get in before me." As he studied her, a soft, bright smile lit his eyes. "Sorry if I've behaved like a brute. It has been a rather difficult morning at the House. I shouldn't have said those things about Gresham."

"I'm sure his book is thrilling."

"Oh, no, it's a dead loss. Murray has read it. I meant the remarks about his age. Personal comments are never in good taste. The poor blighter can't help it if he came off the ark."

"Before you betray your lack of breeding by any more slights on my *friend*, I shall relieve you of the fear you might meet him this evening by informing you he's to attend a lecture." She rose and gave him her hand. "Thank you for taking me to the rout, Montaigne. It will be very useful material."

"You might even enjoy yourself," he suggested.

"Yes indeed. There is nothing I enjoy so much as working. And this afternoon I shall be spying out the secrets of Bond Street. Papa gave me fifty pounds, and Anne and I between us scraped together another fifty, so my pockets are deep. I may even buy myself something."

This speech sounded so pathetic that Montaigne felt like an ogre for having ripped up at her. This trip to London was Sissie's higher education, her university. He was suddenly happy for her that it had been prolonged.

"I shall call for you at three," he said and took his leave, feeling somewhat reassured. Sissie was seeing Gresham only to help with her writing. "Working" she called it. No harm in that. Montaigne was being a dog in the manger, trying to deprive her of her opportunity. He'd point out all the Incomparables to her at the rout and introduce her to the more amusing rakes and rattles. No chance of that mawworm Gresham being at Lady Radcliffe's, at least.

It did not occur to him that the Duke and Duchess of Morland might be there. He met them everywhere, and was beginning to overcome the sense of *gêne* at the encounters, but with Sissie's sharp eyes to scout out his secret, he hoped to avoid the Morlands.

Chapter Ten

When a minor crisis arose at Whitehall that afternoon, Brougham called a meeting of the Whig shadow cabinet. After Montaigne's dereliction that morning, he didn't feel he could miss it. He wrote a note apologizing to Cicely and postponing the trip to Bond Street until the next day. She was relieved to receive it. The sky was overcast, and between riding out with Gresham in the morning and the rout in the evening, she hadn't left herself any time to work on the pantomime.

What she had in mind was a comical piece in which the hero was against Christmas, and his dame contrived all the usual decorations, food, and festivities by a series of pretexts and excuses that became more ludicrous as the piece progressed. This allowed for musical numbers by the carolers and a bit of comedy by the mummers. It would end with the usual Christmas dinner in a fully decorated dining room, with the hero, played by a lady, assuring his dame that Christmas was all humbug. They had had a perfectly fine day without all that stuff and nonsense.

Once Cicely began work, the thing fairly wrote itself. She had a rough copy by five o'clock. Another day or two to polish it and add some more jokes, and she could give it to Mr. Palin in plenty of time for rehearsals on Monday. She was in buoyant spirits for the rout party that evening.

The Fairlys were also in good spirits, anticipating another performance as invalid and nurse. When his wife was courting him, as she was on the evening of Lady Radcliffe's rout party, Fairly paid little heed to other ladies. Had the rout occurred during one of their tiffs, he would have been enchanted with Cicely's appearance.

She wore her chestnut locks drawn to one side, tethered with a white rosebud. Curls bounced saucily against her shoulder. The peach-colored gown of Italian crape with the silver net overskirt, which she borrowed from her hostess, looked quite ravishing on her. With Anne's small string of diamonds to add the final touch of glitter, Cicely was all the crack.

Fairly scarcely glanced at her, but when Lord Montaigne arrived, he looked across the room at the apparition, came to a dead stop, and stared in blatant admiration tinged with astonishment.

"Don't look like that!" Cicely scowled, when he advanced to make his bow. "I know I look abandoned, but all of Meg's gowns are like this."

"Strange, they never looked like this on Meg," he murmured.

"Sissie has done us proud, has she not, Monty?" Meg said. "I shan't blush to sponsor her into Society."

"*I* shall blush like a blue pig!" Sissie said, glancing unhappily at the fulsome expanse of bosom above her gown.

"If you could contrive to be less conscious of your—er, bodice," Montaigne said, caught between a frown and a grin, "then others will not be so aware of it. Remember Lady Godiva."

"I expect you're right. Once I am among other seminude ladies, I shan't feel so exposed."

They had a glass of sherry and were off to Lady Radcliffe's. Montaigne took Cicely in his carriage, as the Fairlys had spoken of darting along to a couple of other dos after they had exhausted the admiration of the Radcliffe party.

Cicely gazed all about at the elegant West End mansions as they drove along to Half Moon Street. When they reached their destination, she made a mental note of the torches flaming in front of the house to lighten the guests' path. The entrance hall, decked out like a summer flower garden—and for only a simple rout—left her speechless.

"I am the only lady here not wearing a fur wrap!" she whispered to Montaigne when he helped her remove her woolen pelisse.

"Fortunate you don't have to wear your wrap into the ballroom. No one will know."

"They will notice I am the only lady wearing chicken-skin arms. It was chilly outside."

As her arms looked fine to Montaigne, he took her remark for a case of the jitters.

When they entered the ballroom, Cicely had to make a conscious effort to keep her mouth closed. She had never seen so many precious jewels, such expanses of silks and satins and female flesh, so many quizzing glasses lifted to examine her until she felt like the bearded lady at the traveling fair. Nor had she ever smelled such a stifling miasma of heady perfumes, all aromas competing to overpower the olfactory sense.

"The assembly at home is nothing to this," she

said in an awed voice, as she gazed around like a regular Johnny Raw.

Montaigne inclined his head to hers and inquired softly, "Do you still feel nude?"

"Ye-e-es," she said uncertainly, "but at least I look like the other ladies. I should feel like a complete dowd if I had worn a decent, modest gown."

The cotillion was in progress when they arrived, so that their first moments were spent mixing with other guests who had come late. Before long, Cicely's attention was caught by a young lady so startlingly beautiful she took the breath away. Hair with the jetty iridescence of a crow's wing swept back from a noble brow. The complexion was ivory, tinged with pale rose on the full cheeks. Cherry-ripe lips opened to reveal a set of perfect pearly teeth. A sequin-spangled gown of white lent an angelic touch to the vision. One felt there ought to be wings sprouting from her shoulders. Cicely couldn't detect the color of the eyes from across the room, though she could see they were large and wide set.

She tugged at Montaigne's elbow and asked, "Who is that beguiling creature with the little man in the burgundy jacket?"

Monty followed her glance across the room. When he beheld the Duchess of Morland, his body stiffened. "The gentleman with her is her husband. They're the Morlands," he said, trying for a tone of indifference.

"You cannot mean she is married to that little ankle-biter with the bulging eyes!"

"Yes. You haven't met the Dartmores, Sissie. Let me introduce you to them." He quickly moved her along the room.

His ruse failed. No sooner were they in conversation with the Dartmores than Cicely resumed the subject of the Morlands. She was having a quiet word with Lady Dartmore while the gentlemen spoke of horses.

"Mrs. Morland is very beautiful, is she not?" she said, gazing across the room.

"Mrs. Morland? I don't seem to recognize the name." Lady Dartmore looked, and beheld Debora. "Oh, you mean the duchess. Yes, she was last Season's Incomparable." She lowered her voice and added, "But perhaps we ought not to discuss her in front of Montaigne."

Comprehension dawned in a flash. "Just so," she said and, at the first opportunity, drew Montaigne away to tease him.

"Would you like to leave, Montaigne?" she asked, feigning concern, but her sparkling eyes alerted him to mischief.

"Leave? We just arrived. We haven't had a dance yet."

"To be sure, but *she* is here."

He gave her a belligerent stare. "I shan't add to your amusement by pretending I don't know whom you're talking about. Of course Debora is here. The Morlands go everywhere."

So that was her name: Debora. "It was very brave of you to come, and I do appreciate it. Do you think you are up to presenting me to her?"

"Why do you want to meet her?" he asked irritably.

"Use your head, Montaigne. Where else am I likely to see amethyst eyes? They are as rare as three-legged hens. I wouldn't miss it for a wilderness of monkeys."

To refuse would only add to her curiosity and lend

a misleading seriousness to his past history with Debora. But they would do no more than say good evening.

"Very well," he said, bracing himself for the ordeal.

He took Cicely's elbow and led her around the corner and down the far wall until he came to the Morlands. While he presented Cicely, she made the proper greetings, but her attention was all on the famous eyes. They were exactly as the author of *Chaos* had described Eugenie's eyes. They changed from violet to a shadowy indigo, depending on the light. The duchess's voice, too, had that same zephyr-like quality often mentioned in the book. Cicely would have called it a little girl's voice. It was high-pitched and so light one had to listen closely to catch her words. Once caught, they hardly seemed worth the bother. She uttered nothing but the most common banalities.

"Charmed to make your acquaintance, Miss Cicely," she said while her gaze fluttered over Cicely's shoulder to Montaigne.

His effort to walk on to another couple failed. Morland had latched on to Cicely. As they all stood talking, Cicely noticed that the duchess's hands fluttered like butterflies—just as Eugenie's hands fluttered. Other little things, too, reinforced the likeness. She had a beauty spot on the left corner of her chin. Eugenie's was on the right corner, but taken altogether, the similarities were too striking to have occurred by chance. The Duchess was Eugenie Beaureport. But there was no way in the world that the duke was the handsome, dashing Lord Ravencroft.

Ere long, the duchess's banalities turned to complaints. The general behavior of the Morlands reminded Cicely forcefully of the Fairlys' before their latest rapprochement.

"I told Morland I didn't want to come here tonight," the sweet voice said. "The Rutlands are having a masquerade party. I had a lovely costume made up." An adorable moue drew her lips into a bow.

"No use for costume parties," Morland said firmly. He had been paying Cicely marked attention. When the dancing stopped, he said, "Miss Cicely, may I have the pleasure of the next set?"

"I should like it. Thank you," she replied, and was led to the floor in hopes of discovering the identity of Lord Ravencroft. It proved beyond Cicely's powers of invention to ask the question, however, as she spent her time fighting off Morland's advances.

Montaigne had taken for granted that he, as Cicely's escort, would have the first set with her. He felt a definite sensation of pique when she left with Morland. And to make it worse, he was now in the position of having to stand up with Debora, with all of Society tittering behind raised fingers and fans. Next they would be saying he had become her lover. It was some small consolation to see that Cicely was not enjoying herself. Even as research material, Morland was useless.

Chapter Eleven

When the set finished, Cicely was swept away with another gentleman. Montaigne, watching from the side of the room, judged she was better entertained by Mr. Witherspoon, an eligible bachelor about town.

Fairly became bored with being an invalid and decided he was cured. He took off his sling and went after Cicely for the next set. Meg stood up with Morland, who had discovered Lady Fairly was the means of access to Miss Cicely, whom he praised with the ambiguous description "a regular little guy." Meg hadn't the least notion what he meant, nor could he elucidate when she asked him.

When supper was announced, the Morlands accompanied the Fairlys, Montaigne, and Cicely to the table.

Morland flirted with Meg; Fairly ogled Cicely and the duchess more or less equally, Montaigne was as close to a fit of sulks as was possible for a gentleman of his years, and Cicely had a marvelous time ferreting out the secrets of Society.

The Prince Regent, she discovered, was having an affair with someone called Lady Hertford, much to the gratification of the lady's husband. Everyone was carrying on with everyone else's spouse. Cicely began to think she had straggled into Sodom and Gomorrah. It seemed the only faithful lady in all of London was someone called Emily, but eventually even Emily disappointed her. It was the lady's lover, not her husband, to whom she was so faithful.

All this disillusionment did not prevent Cicely from watching Montaigne and the duchess. She could discern no overt advances on his part and was forced to the conclusion that only a red-hot affair could account for his flagrant indifference to such compelling temptation.

After a midnight supper, the Fairlys continued on to another rout. Cicely was hagged and asked Montaigne to take her home. He called for his carriage at once.

"You were right to speak of the fleshpots of London, Montaigne," she said, drawing her gloved hand across her forehead. "I had no idea there was so much debauchery in the world. Is no one faithful to his wife in this city?"

"We know no ill of the king, in that respect," he replied. "Unlike his sons."

"But the rest of them . . ."

"There are many good marriages. Those unfashionable folks are not spoken of. Who would listen if one said Lord Eldon went home to his wife every evening?"

"I'm monstrously relieved to hear it. And now I should like to speak of something closer to home. About the Duchess of Morland . . ."

Montaigne schooled his voice to indifference. "Well, you have met her. What do you think?"

"I think you were fortunate she jilted you. One can see how you were bowled over by her appearance. She is quite the loveliest creature I have ever seen, but not much to say for herself. Of course I expect the fact that your affair now has to be clandestine adds a certain element of romance and danger, but—"

"My affair!"

"Well, you are seeing her, aren't you?"

"Certainly not!"

"Really?" She squinted suspiciously in the darkness. "From the way you never looked within a right angle of her, I made sure you two were carrying on a madly passionate affair."

"I am shocked at you, Sissie!"

"Doing it too brown, Montaigne. How can anyone who spends so much time in London be shocked by anything? Even the Prince Regent—imagine!"

"Especially the Prince Regent."

"And they say his mistress isn't even pretty."

"One soon tires of a pretty face."

"Or even a beautiful one. The duke is bored with his duchess already. And by the by, he is a shocking flirt."

"I noticed," Montaigne said through thinning lips.

"Meg says he called me 'a regular little guy.' What does that mean, Montaigne? I believe he meant it as a compliment."

Montaigne assumed its real meaning was that she was different from Debora. As he wished to avoid any mention of that young lady, however, he said, "I expect it means outspoken and intelligent without any girlish tricks, yet still dashed pretty." He peered to see how she reacted to this ducal compliment.

"It is no compliment to be thought intelligent by *him*," she scoffed.

"Surely he must be allowed to know a pretty face at least. After all, he did marry Debora."

"I rather think she married him."

"That is implicit in his marrying her, *n'est-ce pas?*"

"It's not the same thing at all. He's the harum-scarum sort who could have been nabbed by any determined lady. I think she just wanted to be a duchess."

"And I think her mama wanted to be a duchess's mama, but I take your point. You did not take mine, however. I was trying to compliment your pretty face."

"My pretty face thanks you," she said airily.

Montaigne found it difficult to continue his flirtation in this inhospitable climate. They drove along in silence. When they alighted at Berkeley Square, a wind had arisen, a cold wind that spoke of winter's approach. It whipped Cicely's mantle about and pulled at her curls.

Montaigne took her elbow. "Come, let us get inside before you develop chicken skin."

"Is that snow?" she asked. A few stray flakes blew against her cheeks. They caught in her hair, where they glistened like diamonds in the moonlight.

"The first of the season. Not a real snowfall," Montaigne said, glancing up to read the luminous sky. Then he looked at Cicely and felt a strange warmth grow inside him. How lovely she looked in the semidarkness, with her big eyes shining. Like a phantom lady in a romance.

"A cup of tea would be nice," she said, huddling into her cape as she hastened up the stairs, unaware of his mood. "If it wasn't so late, I'd ask you in."

"It's only one o'clock," he said.

"Only! Good gracious, if I were at home, I would have been snoring for three hours by now. But I don't feel tired, somehow. I expect I'm too excited from the rout."

Montaigne flickered a glance at her. Her quaint views and her blunt manner of talking about "snoring" brought a fleeting smile to his lips. A phantom lady should speak more elegantly.

"When in Rome," he reminded her.

"Tomorrow's a working day." She looked at him. "Well, are you coming in or not?"

He took this ambiguous invitation as encouragement and replied, "That was my intention."

The butler opened the door for them. Montaigne asked for tea, and they went into the saloon. Cicely looked surprised when he sat beside her on the sofa, instead of in one of the chairs.

"You must get at your script as soon as I bring you home from Bond Street tomorrow," he said. "Mustn't miss that important research. Do you have an idea yet for the pantomime?"

"Oh, I have it written. I just have to polish it," she replied.

"Finished! When did you find time to do it?"

"I had the whole afternoon free, you recall. Tomorrow morning I shall polish it, and tomorrow afternoon we go to Bond Street." As she spoke, she removed the clasp from her hair. "You don't mind my dishabille?" she asked. "Perkins made the barrette so tight it's giving me the megrims. What a horrid chore it is, trying to look stylish."

She ran her fingers through her hair to relieve the scalp irritation of the barrette. Montaigne studied her, trying to decide whether she looked prettier with the cluster of curls on her shoulder or with her hair all tousled up, as it was now. The carefree style suited her better.

"I expect you were pretty cut up when the duchess married Morland," Cicely said leadingly.

"Let us speak of something else," Montaigne said testily. He had had quite enough of the duchess for one night.

She reached out and patted his hand. Montaigne felt a little ripple of pleasure at the implied intimacy of it.

"I understand, Montaigne," she said. "But really, you know, it is for the best. You'll get over her eventually. Morland is over her already. He invited me to Hastings for a huge Christmas party they are having. Can you imagine! I scarcely know them. If anyone invited me, it ought to have been the duchess. As if I would go anywhere but home for Christmas. He had the most lecherous light in his eye!"

Montaigne felt such a murderous rage, he could hardly contain himself. "The sooner you turn that script over to Palin and go home, the better," he said, and splashed too much milk into his tea cup.

"Yes, I should like to be home at least a week before Christmas, to help Anne with the preparations."

"That's weeks away! It's only the beginning of December!"

"My, you do sound eager to see the back of me. You are forgetting the rehearsals. Mr. Palin mentioned that I ought to be available for a week after the pantomime goes into rehearsal, in case they require revisions. I hope to get away by the middle of December, but definitely by the eighteenth. Meanwhile there is ever so much research to be done.

That nice Mr. Witherspoon offered to take me to Bedlam."

"Why do you want to go and gawk at the lunatics?"

"That's not why I want to go! I just want to see what it's like, in case I ever want to write about it. Everyone says you ought to write about what you know, and I don't know anything. Except village life, I mean." She drew a frustrated sigh. "I daresay I would learn all sorts of interesting things at Morland's Christmas party. Pity it is a Christmas party."

"You're already going to Bedlam. There is no need to go to Morland's."

She gave him a cool stare. "I doubt the lunatics at Bedlam enjoy their confinement in ducal style."

As Cicely had decided not to attend, Montaigne didn't bother to discourage her further. They had another cup of tea and spoke of other things. His suggestion of driving all around London to see the various quarters found favor. London was growing like a mushroom, with new homes sprouting up overnight.

"I'm sure Meg will lend me her carriage," she said. "John Groom will know where to take me."

"I will take you," Montaigne said.

"I shan't encroach on your time. You've hinted often enough I am overstaying my welcome."

"I'm sorry if I gave you that impression. It is just that I am a little concerned for the sort of company you are meeting."

"Why, Monty! You don't trust me! You think I will fall into a hobble! You needn't worry. I can take care of myself."

But when he remembered the duke's invitation to

Hastings for a house party, and how Fairly had botched the trip to Seven Dials, he was adamant.

"I will take you," he repeated.

He left as soon as the tea had been drunk. Cicely was already yawning into her fist. She went up to her bed immediately, but as she lay thinking over her unusual evening, she remembered something that had escaped her during all the excitement. How had Montaigne's Aunt Ethel written such an accurate description of Debora when she had never seen her? Debora was Eugenie; of that there could be no doubt. Montaigne was trying to conceal the real author. Why, he hadn't even remembered Ethel's name. He had called her Irma. Whom was he trying to protect? The book was nothing else but a eulogy to Debora. If the author was a friend of hers, she wouldn't have to hide it.

Actually, the descriptions had rather the air of a lover's rant. No doubt Debora had dozens of suitors, Montaigne among them. Cicely suddenly sat bolt upright. Of course! Monty had written the book himself! That was why he drew back his ears like an angry mare every time she disparaged it. And that was why he was so eager to conceal the author's true identity. Good God! How his colleagues would stare if they ever learned the truth. The white hope of the Whig Party was a romancer. A wicked smile lifted her lips as she lay down again. What fun! A gurgle of laughter echoed in the dark room. Aunt Ethel indeed!

Chapter Twelve

Cicely was an early riser. An advantage to rising early at the Fairlys' was that she had left the breakfast table long before her hostess was up. She would have enjoyed some privacy with Meg, but Meg usually took breakfast in bed.

Cicely spent the morning polishing her pantomime. By noon she was satisfied with it and sent it off with a footman to Mr. Palin, at Covent Garden. When she glanced out the window to judge the weather, she saw the sky was gray, but not the dark, ominous gray that threatened rain or snow. She would wear her woolen pelisse for the trip along Bond Street, and a plainish bonnet, as the wind would tear any feathers from their moorings. To add a note of style to the low poke, Anne, who was handy with a needle, had added a fur lining to the brim and lent Cicely her best beaver muff. The muff had a small sealed compartment to hold money, thus avoiding the necessity of borrowing a reticule from Meg.

As she prepared for the outing, Cicely thought of the lovely time she would have ragging Montaigne about his authorship of *Chaos*.

"Surely you are not taking Cicely out in this gale!" Meg exclaimed when Montaigne came to call. She was entertaining half a dozen ladies in her saloon. The ostensible occupation was cards, but the real job was gossip. After her success in the matter of Fairly's invalidism, Meg had ventured down another original path. She planned to serve the ladies apple tart made from Cicely's apples. Cook had already made one, which had turned out well. Why not, if that French queen—or was it a courtesan—could make her friends milk cows?

"It's all right, Meg. I wore my woolen pelisse," Cicely told her.

"Woolen? My dear, the wind will cut straight through wool. Does it have a fur lining?"

"There is some fur," Cicely said vaguely, thinking of her muff. She was becoming embarrassed at having to borrow so many of her hostess's clothes.

Montaigne noticed that Sissie was looking particularly lively that day. He assumed it was anticipation of the visit to Bond Street that accounted for it. It struck him that her vivacity made Meg's set look like painted corpses. Their only color came out of the rouge pot.

When he helped Cicely on with her woolen pelisse, she pointed to the beaver muff. "I didn't say where the fur was," she admitted. "I feel like a cheapskate, always borrowing from Meg. Is it very cold out?"

"Not terribly cold, but windy. I have a fur rug in the carriage."

"If it's too chilly, I can throw it around me for a shawl," she laughed. "Start a new style. Meg thinks she's being original by serving her guests apple tart this afternoon. I don't know where she got the idea that's something new. We have it at least once a week at Elmdale."

"The novelty is introducing a touch of country into the city menu," he explained.

"Perhaps my country duds will set a new style," she said, but her offhand manner told him she didn't really care what folks thought of her wardrobe.

He was coming to realize it was morals rather than manners that interested her. A surprising number of the ton didn't appear to know the difference. Any debauchery was acceptable, so long as it was executed with style.

"I think not, Sissie. You are unique," he said, and bowed.

"The worst-dressed creature in London, you mean," she scowled.

"On the contrary. You are the only lady who has the bravura to carry off that bonnet successfully."

She studied him suspiciously. "I shall look that word up in the dictionary as soon as I get home. I thought it had something to do with music."

"I shall save you the trouble. It was a compliment."

"Oh, in that case I shall tell Anne. She put in the fur lining."

He arranged the fur rug over her knees and they were off. Cicely was about to introduce the subject of his novel, *Chaos*, when Montaigne spoke on a different matter that also interested her greatly.

"I had a note from Murray this morning," he mentioned. "He's eager to see *Georgiana*. Has Gresham returned the manuscript yet?"

"Not yet. He hasn't had it long. I cannot expect him to ignore his own important work. I am dying to know what Murray thinks, though. If Sir Giles doesn't return it soon, I shall ask him for it. I'd like Murray's decision before I leave London. If he takes it, I might buy a fur-lined cape. They look so cozy, and I need a new winter cape. Are they very dear?"

"You won't get much under a hundred pounds."

Her bright eyes blinked in astonishment. "Good Lord! That much, just for a couple of pelts?"

Montaigne's lips moved in amusement. "They come all the way from Canada," he explained.

"They must all be rich as Croesus in Canada if they get that kind of money for their furs. I have half a mind to skin a couple of foxes and let Anne make the lining herself. I daresay she could do it. She's very handy with her needle."

As they entered Bond Street, her chatter ceased. She gazed in stupefaction at the storefronts and the members of the ton who had braved the wind to go on the strut. "Can we get out and walk now?" she asked.

Montaigne drew the drawstring and they alighted. "You're looking very sparkish today, Sissie," he said.

"I did some thinking last night," she said with a long, meaningful look at him. "About your Aunt Irma, who has never seen the duchess. Odd how she described her to a T. Even the mole on her chin."

"Beauty mark!"

"I shall make a note of that. On a duchess a mole is called a beauty mark. Don't try to divert me, Montaigne. I've figured the whole thing out."

He felt a jolt of shock but assumed he could talk his way out of it. "I was mistaken about Aunt Irma's not having met Debora. Auntie does come to town occasionally. I recall she was here last winter to visit a doctor, now that I think of it."

"Along with your Aunt Ethel?" Cicely asked with a conning smile.

"Ethel?" he asked uncertainly. He had a vague

123

memory of some confusion as to the imaginary lady's name earlier.

"You said it was your Aunt Ethel, from Cornwall, who wrote the book. I asked Meg if she ever got to Cornwall to visit her aunt. She says she has no aunt in Cornwall. You didn't coach her properly, Montaigne. You ought to have known she'd require hours of instruction. I've caught you dead to rights, sir. You wrote that load of mush." She burst into whoops of laughter, right in the middle of Bond Street.

He took a close grip on her arm. "Behave yourself! People are looking at you."

"Let them look. It's you they'd be staring at if they ever knew the truth. Lord Montaigne, the clever parliamentarian—and anonymous lady who wrote *Chaos Is Come Again.*"

Montaigne felt as if a deep, dark pit had suddenly opened before him. Ridicule, laughter, utter ruin for his career. He'd never be taken seriously again. He could forget being a minister when the Whigs took power.

"Shut up!" he cried, then stared around in horror as he realized what he had said—to a lady, on busy Bond Street. A passerby gave him a rebukeful look and shook his head. "I'm sorry, Sissie."

"I wager you never spoke to Eugenie like that," she said, and laughed again. "The purple pools would turn to waterfalls if you ever raised your voice to her. Oh, Monty! How *could* you? I took you for a sensible gentleman."

The clever parliamentarian resumed control. He ushered Cicely into the farthest corner of a shop devoid of customers to reason with her. He would appeal to her sympathy. Sissie was a good-hearted, sensible girl. She'd understand.

"It's true I wrote the book," he said and continued to speak earnestly and at length. "I was under some mental stress at the time. Things going badly at Whitehall, and me laid up with that painful busted ankle, unable to help. Just the worst time of year for a broken heart—spring. The doctor suggested I needed a diversion. I began the thing as a mental exercise to ease the stress. After it had grown into a hundred pages, I took the notion that I might make some money for the orphans if I finished it and sold it."

She looked and listened, then spoke. "That might do if you had written a different book," she said. "But what you wrote was that silly pudding of a thing about Debora. You'd be laughed out of town if it ever came out, Montaigne."

"I know it well. You've got to help me, Sissie. I'll— I'll buy you that fur-lined cape you want."

She drew in a sharp breath and turned on him like a virago. "How dare you try to bribe me! If you had told me the truth from the beginning, if you had trusted me, I could laugh and take it in good spirit, but to use me like this! Lie to me! Lumber me with that farrago because you're ashamed to admit you wrote it yourself. It is really the outside of enough, Montaigne. I took you for an honest man. I thought there was one person in wicked London I could always trust."

"Serpent's tooth! You *can* trust me."

"It looks like it! How do I know you're even giving the money to charity?"

"I can show you the receipt. You've seen for yourself how badly the money is needed."

She believed he was donating the proceeds to charity and admired him for it but was not through quizzing him yet. "Do you know, Monty, I wager you'd sell thousands more copies if people knew *you* had written it. Every M.P. would buy a book, and another to give to his friends."

His face froze in horror. "Sissie, you wouldn't! You can't!"

"We shall see," she said.

The proprietor came forward and Cicely began to look over his wares. She bought a new snuff box for her papa, and a pretty little silver pin box for Anne. Montaigne watched, planning how he could prevent her from revealing his secret. Why hadn't he told her the truth from the beginning? He should have made her secrecy a part of their bargain. Too late now. He was faced with the galling knowledge that whatever terms she set, he would have to abide by them.

He forced a sickly smile and ushered her from the shop. "Where would you like to go next?"

"I have to get Anne's blue stockings. She'd have my head if I went home without them. And a graduated beaker for Cook."

Montaigne, who abhorred loitering about ladies' shops, spent the next half hour doing just that. While Cicely pondered the wisdom of buying two blue pairs versus one blue and one dark green to go with Anne's green gown, Montaigne's mind was on his own problem. He couldn't bribe Sissie with money, but perhaps he could perform some favor in regard to her own novel. If Murray hated it, for instance, he would offer to publish it for her.

They continued on for another half hour, visiting a dozen shops of all sorts. Montaigne had not realized the range of merchandise from all over the world that was available in London. If he had not been so upset, he would have been bored witless. He didn't see how his afternoon could possibly be any worse, but when he saw the Morlands strolling toward them, he knew he was mistaken.

The instant Morland spotted them, he came rushing forward, dragging Debora with him. "By Jove, just the folks I was looking for," he said and bowed. "Debbie and I have been talking over that house party, Miss Cicely. Demmed shame you can't come to us for Christmas. Love to have you. And you, too, Montaigne. We've come up with a solution. We'll have a do next weekend as well. You can come to us then. Won't take no for an answer."

"I'm afraid I'll be busy. Government business," Montaigne said vaguely.

"Pity," Morland said and returned his attention to Sissie. "I know you ain't busy, Miss Cicely, for we stopped at Fairly's, and Meg has already accepted. Told us we would find you on Bond Street. Said you had nothing on for the weekend. It's all set, then. Next Friday, just for a few days. We'll return Tuesday or Wednesday, just as you like. Hastings. Meg knows where it is. Nowhere near Hastings the city. It's much handier to Town. In Kent, near Maidstone. Only a hop away." He remembered his wife and said to her, "That's right, eh, Debbie?"

"We would love to have you, Miss Cicely," she said dutifully. Her amethyst orbs turned to Montaigne. "I'm sorry you can't join us, Montaigne."

"Actually, Miss Cicely won't be able to get away, either," he said. "She is writing a Christmas pantomime for Palin."

"Yes, she told us all about it," Morland said.

"Dash it, they can't expect her to be on hand for days on end only for a pantomime. I'll fix it up with Palin, if need be. Won't take no for an answer."

Montaigne turned a fiery eye on Cicely. "I'm afraid you must decline," he said firmly.

This was too much for Cicely. "I should love to go, Your Grace. I'm sure my Aunt Ethel won't mind," she said, directing her words to the duchess, who was not curious enough to inquire what her Aunt Ethel had to do with it.

"Lovely," Debora said. Her attention had already wandered to a shop window. She nudged the duke's elbow and said, "Look, Dickie! Mademoiselle Françoise has some new bonnets in her window."

Morland was so pleased with his success that he allowed himself to be led off to buy his wife yet another bonnet.

Montaigne leveled a cold stare on his companion. "Shall we go home now, Miss Cicely?"

"Certainly, Lord Montaigne, for I am feeling a little chilly without a fur cape. Did you see the gorgeous lining in the duchess's? Russian sable, I wager."

"I offered to buy you one!"

"We shall forget that piece of impertinence, or I shall have to be angry with you, and I don't want to. I have had a splendid afternoon, and I thank you for not saying all the horrid things you have been wanting to say. I wonder what can account for it?" she asked innocently.

He realized then that she had known all along what a horrible time she was subjecting him to while she loitered over the graduated beakers. And she had enjoyed every minute of it.

"Wretch!" he growled.

"Feeling colicky, Aunt Ethel? Never mind; at least you won't have to spend the weekend at Hastings."

"And that's another thing! You're not going there!"

"And where should I go instead, if Meg and Fairly are going? I can hardly move into your bachelor establishment, or even a hotel, without a chaperon."

"I'll speak to Meg. She can make some excuse."

"We are going, Montaigne. But there is one crumb of satisfaction in it for you. It is halfway to Elmdale. I shall finish up any business of the pantomime with Mr. Moore before I leave, and return home to Elmdale from Hastings. You won't have to worry about my revealing any embarrassing secrets."

Montaigne knew he had been bested. And on top of it all, he would now have to eat humble pie. Call on the Morlands and say he had arranged to get the weekend off. His friends and colleagues would have a fine time ranting at him for the indiscretion of spending a weekend with the Morlands, when gossip hinted of trouble between them. Whatever it took, he damned well wasn't going to let Sissie attend one of the Morlands' wild weekends with only the Fairlys for chaperons.

Chapter Thirteen

Over the next days, Montaigne was kept busy at Whitehall, arguing bills the Tories were trying to ram through without sufficient debate before the Christmas recess. Despite his busy schedule, he called several times at Berkeley Square. On each occasion, Miss Cicely and Lady Fairly were out. When he finally found them in on the fourth day, he hardly recognized Sissie. Her long hair had been shorn. What remained covered her head in a cap of bouncing curls. Her toilette was different, too. The navy gown she wore was modest enough, but it was not the sort of gown he was accustomed to see her wear at Elmdale. It was less ornate and more stylish.

She arose and turned all around. "What do you think? Will it do?" she asked with a certain eagerness that pleased him.

His first angry instinct was to say she looked wretched, but a second look told him the new style suited her uncommonly well. The saucy coiffure added to her gamine charm. "Very nice," he allowed.

"Do you really like it? Meg's French modiste made it for me. And the coiffure is called the Cheribime. Anne thought, when we saw it in the *Ladies Maga-*

zine, that it would suit me. It's easy to care for. I don't have to put papers in at night."

"That's—er, convenient," Montaigne said uncertainly. He was more interested to discover what important business had kept her away from the house all week. "I hope you haven't forgotten business in all the rush of becoming a dasher."

The ladies had been having an informal tea in the saloon when he arrived. Meg poured him a cup and passed him a piece of gingerbread.

"I'm pretty well finished with Moore. We've been shopping, visiting milliners and modistes, and, in the evening, darting about to parties," Sissie announced, with such a beatific smile that Montaigne hadn't the heart to chastise her. She had come to London to see how the ton behaved, and she was seeing it firsthand. "It's been so lovely!" she said, her dark eyes glowing.

"We discovered the party at Hastings is going to be very grand," Meg told him. "Close to a hundred guests. Every spare room full. Naturally for such a grand visit, Sissie had to buy a few things and have a new gown made up for the ball."

"Ball?"

"Yes, the Morlands are having a grand ball at Hastings," Meg said. "It is the half-year anniversary of their wedding. Dickie is keeping it a secret from Debbie, but he is having a special ball for her on the Saturday. He has been here half a dozen times discussing it with us."

Montaigne's lips thinned and his nostrils flared. He shot a scowling look at Sissie, who ignored it. "Surely it is himself who should be making the arrangements. I wouldn't have thought it would take half a dozen visits, in any case."

131

"It's more than just the ball, actually," Meg explained. "There is to be a musical evening as well. He has hired London musicians to perform. Sissie is helping Dick write new words for 'Greensleeves.' He's going to sing it at the concert, as a sort of tribute to Debora. Of course he cannot practice it at home, or she'll hear him, so he drops in here mornings. I play the pianoforte for him."

At least Meg was here to play propriety, for what that was worth. "Where were you last evening? I stopped by after the session, around nine."

"Last night? Now, let me see . . . Spencer's musical evening, was it? No, that was the night before. Oh yes, of course. Cousin Sabina had us to dinner, and one of those tedious games evenings after. Not even cards, but word games."

"I won first prize," Sissie said. She lifted an old-fashioned painted chicken-skin fan to show him. "Second prize was a box of bonbons. I would have preferred that."

Montaigne had declined Sabina's invitation, hoping to take Cicely to a livelier do. If she must be jauntering about without him, a musical evening and one of Cousin Sabina's games evenings were exactly the outings he could approve.

"Excellent. That would be good research for you, Sissie."

"Yes, I want to know the boring things as well as the exciting ones," she said earnestly.

"If you're free tomorrow morning, we can begin the tours of London," he suggested.

"Thank you, Montaigne, but Mr. Witherspoon is taking me to Bedlam tomorrow," she replied.

"And this evening?" he asked, reining his temper.

"The Morlands have invited us to Drury Lane with them."

"You are seeing a great deal of the Morlands!"

"More of Dick than Debora, actually," Meg said. "She has been feeling poorly, but she will be with us tonight."

Fairly arrived and occupied Meg's attention with some new gossip he had picked up at Brooks's. Montaigne took the opportunity for some private conversation with Cicely.

"Has Gresham sent back *Georgiana* yet?" he asked.

"He brought it this morning," she said, frowning.

Montaigne's heart leaped with hope. "He didn't care for it?" This was his chance to make up to Sissie for his poor behavior. Though Gresham's disapproval didn't necessarily mean the book was unpublishable.

"I really can't tell. He said it showed great promise, but went on with so many niggling complaints that I feel I ought to throw it in the grate and start over. He wants me to take out my favorite parts. He says good writing doesn't have to resort to low humor. He meant the pig getting loose in the garden, I expect. He's offered to help me work on it." The slump of her shoulders told him Gresham's complaints had depressed her. "That was very kind of him, was it not?"

"Monstrously kind!" he said angrily. "He wants to hack at it and make it as dull as his own outpourings. Let me show it to Murray before you go changing it."

"After talking to Gresham, I'm ashamed to let anyone read it." A mischievous gleam twinkled in

133

her eyes. "Though Murray *did* publish *Chaos*," she added.

"You haven't told anyone?" he asked anxiously.

"Of course not—yet."

"If you would just let me explain, Sissie. I only did it for a lark. I had been reading *The Castle of Otranto.* I thought it might be a good chance to hone my own writing—for speeches in the House and an occasional political article. I was ill, recuperating from that busted ankle."

"And a busted heart. That is why you subjected Eugenie to such horrid tribulations. It was revenge for Debora's jilting you."

"Naturally she was much on my mind at that time. She had just accepted the duke's offer."

"Now I begin to understand you. Under that cool facade you are a dangerous romantic lunatic, Montaigne. Thank God you do not care for me in that way."

"I was suffering from melancholia! I wasn't myself."

"No, you were Baron Ravencroft. Never give more than one explanation. Such a plethora of them sounds like excuses."

"I expect you think Ravencroft was a jackass."

Her teasing expression softened into a fond smile. "Strange, now that you mention it, I didn't pay much attention to the baron. He was not so bad as Eugenie. In fact, he was rather sweet, in a maudlin sort of way. Did you really press that perfect red rose Eug—Debora gave you and sleep with it under your pillow?"

"It was only a violet," he said, blushing. "I put it between the leaves of a book, but when I lent the book to Meg, I took it out. It broke apart. The small gesture has to be enhanced and romanticized for fiction."

"Not if you're writing about Dickie. He asked me to call him Dickie. Imagine me being on a first-name basis with a duke! I feel I shall have to tone down his excesses, or no one would credit them. I'm planning a marvelous fool based on him for my next novel. Of course I won't be able to call him a duke. Pity, for a prince doesn't fit my story. I shall have to demote him to a marquess. Do you know what he suggested, Montaigne?"

Her shocked face gave rise to the worst possible ideas. Montaigne came to rigid attention. Such outré suggestions as a ménage à trois occurred to him. Was he to be involved in a duel? "Imagination fails," he said in a thin voice.

"He invited me to go to Italy with him and Debora next spring."

"What!"

"With, of course, a whole retinue of chaperons and couriers and his very own doctor and a coiffeur for the ladies and I don't know what all. Did you ever hear anything so extravagant in your life? It would be a wonderful experience. And he meant it! He was going to pay for everything, too."

"I trust you did not encourage this folly!"

"Unfortunately, I couldn't. I can just imagine Papa's howls if I suggested such a thing. To say nothing of Debora's. Really he is the outside of enough. But pure gold for research purposes. Twenty-four carat. The minute he leaves, I dart to my notebook to jot down what he said."

Montaigne felt his annoyance melting when he discovered the nature of her interest in Morland. A

135

lady wasn't likely to go tumbling into love with someone she considered a buffoon.

"I expect you'll sneak a small notebook into Anne's muff when you visit the theater this evening," he said.

"But of course. I shall let on I'm making notes on the play. Since I wrote the pantomime, Morland has taken the notion I never stop scribbling. He asked me if I had published any books this week." A silvery tinkle of laughter erupted.

"You say you have spoken to Moore about your pantomime?"

"Yes, and he liked it. He doesn't foresee many changes. I shall go to one rehearsal to smooth out any lines that give the characters trouble. Palin paid me a hundred pounds for the copyright! I've squandered half of it already. You have no notion how expensive it is for a lady to keep in fashion."

"Do I not? And by the by, you should never sell the copyright, but as it's only a short sketch, it is no matter."

"As you are familiar with the price of ladies' fashion, then I assume you do have a bit o' muslin? I asked Meg, but she—"

"I did not say how I knew. You forget I have a sister." His dark eyes dared her to continue this discussion.

"So you have, and don't think I mean to pester you about your light-o'-love, for I know it is not at all the thing. I can find out from any of Meg's friends, as Meg doesn't know if you ever replaced the opera dancer . . ."

"That was some years ago."

"Well, never mind. I have got quite enough research about how the gentlemen carry on from Meg.

It was nice having this chat, Montaigne. I hope you aren't angry about my going to Hastings, but really, you know, I could not pass up such an opportunity. I never met a duke and duchess before and probably never shall again. I just couldn't refuse. Of course I shan't tell anyone you wrote *Chaos*. I was just teasing you."

"I should have told you the truth from the beginning," he said. His mind lingered on her casual dismissal of his love life. She obviously had no personal interest in it.

"Yes. If I had known, I wouldn't have ragged you so about Eugenie. I know, after Sir Giles's note, how much criticism hurts. It is as if he had taken a scalpel to my child. If I had really despised your book, I wouldn't have read it all the way through—in one sitting," she added, laughing at herself. "I expect it was half jealousy at its popularity that goaded me."

"I never considered it great literature. Speaking of which—shall I take *Georgiana* to Murray this afternoon?"

"I'll get it."

She bounced up and took a parcel from a side table. "Here she is. Guard her with your life. It is the only fair copy I have." She was suddenly sober, almost frightened. She took a deep breath to steady her voice and said, "And Monty, I want you to tell me the truth, whatever Murray says. If it's awful, tell me where I went wrong."

He read the tension in Cicely's voice and realized how important this was to her. He determined on the spot that if Murray hated it, he wouldn't tell her but make some excuse about a crowded publishing schedule and publish it himself.

"I shall ask him to have a quick look at it immediately and give you his first impression at Drury Lane this evening."

A bright smile beamed. "Oh, are you coming?" she asked.

"I'm not invited to join the Morlands' party, but I shall drop in and visit you at intermission."

"Murray won't have time to read my book before the play. That only gives him a few hours. It's three hundred pages."

"He can get an idea of the style, at least."

"Let him read it at his leisure. There is no need for you to make a special trip to Drury Lane. If he hates it, it will spoil the play."

"I have another reason for going. I have to eat some humble pie. You don't think I plan to let you have all of Morland's excesses to yourself? One never knows, I might bust another ankle, and have to write away my pain."

"Do you mean—"

"Yes, I plan to rescind my refusal to the party at Hastings, even though the rooms are all taken. It's close to Christmas, after all. He won't refuse me a couple of chairs and a bolster by the fireplace in the festive season."

"Oh, I am glad you're coming," she said and reached out to seize his hands in hers. When she realized what she had done, she pulled her hands back with a self-conscious start. "Half the fun of all my research is having someone to talk to about it. Until I get home to tell Anne, there's no one. Meg and Fairly don't find the duke very amusing. It has all been so exciting and lovely. I wouldn't have missed it for the world, but in a way, I'm glad it's nearly over. London has changed Meg. I wouldn't want it to do that to me. When I look at myself in the mirror, I hardly recognize me."

"Meg was always a widgeon," he said frankly. "It wouldn't change a stronger character like you. It hasn't changed me, I hope." He paused, lifting an eyebrow in thought, remembering Cicely's anger at learning he had lied about *Chaos*. *"I thought there was one person in wicked London I could always trust,"* she had said. "Do I sound as conceited as I think I do?"

"Yes," she said, "though I suspect there might be a grain of truth in it. You don't seem to have changed much in any case, but I am nearly as excited as Meg about the gown I'm having made up for Morland's ball. It has silver spangles. I never had a gown with spangles before."

"I look forward to seeing it."

"The only disappointment in the visit is that I shan't see my Christmas pantomime performed. I shall be home by then."

A quick frown seized Montaigne's brow. "That's a pity. Could you not stay?"

"I've already stayed longer than I intended. I am expected at Elmdale by the eighteenth at the latest. Will you be in London for Christmas, Montaigne?"

"I'm not sure."

"If you are, will you go to see the pantomime and perhaps, if it wouldn't be too much trouble, send me any little squibs that might be in the journals?"

"Of course. And now I shall rush *Georgiana* off to Murray."

As Montaigne took his leave of Cicely and the Fairlys, his heart felt pounds lighter than when he had arrived, though he was unhappy to think of Sissie's having to miss the debut of her pantomime at Covent Garden. As for the rest of it, he could hardly expect her to sit waiting for him to call when she had come here to see the sights. He was glad she was having such an exciting visit. Even the house party at Hastings offered some prospect of amusement.

He left Cicely on pins and needles. What if Murray hated her book? Sir Giles's critique had cast her into utter gloom. The novel suddenly seemed too trite and silly and provincial to show to a London publisher. But after this visit, she had some inkling of how real Society went on. The next one would be better.

Chapter Fourteen

The play at Drury Lane that evening was a superior performance of *The Way to Keep Him*, by Murphy. Everyone agreed the actress playing Mrs. Lovemore did an excellent job. Mr. Witherspoon, Cicely's escort, was handsome and amusing. The duke, up to his usual height of foolishness, had sent the ladies corsages of orchids and given each a crystal bottle of perfume with a gold stopper as a memento of the evening. Champagne was served at the intermission, and during the performance treats were passed—bonbons, nuts, dried cherries. And through it all, Cicely sat in an agony of suspense, waiting for Montaigne to come.

When Montaigne didn't appear at the first intermission, Cicely was certain Murray had disliked the book, and that Montaigne didn't want to spoil the evening by telling her. When he didn't show up for the second intermission either, suspense caused such an ache between Cicely's temples that she felt almost ill. She didn't hear a single word of the duke's lavish praise of Mrs. Lovemore, which would have made excellent jotting for her notebook.

The duchess, who had yawned and complained of nausea throughout the play, wanted to go home afterward. As the duke had spent his afternoon arranging a special dinner at the Clarendon, he wanted to take his guests on there.

"Ah, here is Montaigne!" he said. "He can take Debora home, and we'll go on for dinner. You don't mind, Debbie?"

At the word "Montaigne," Cicely's heart turned to ice. She glanced to the doorway of the box, where Montaigne had just entered. She tried to read by his expression what had transpired at Murray's, but the shadowy box defeated her. It was too dark to see the excitement glowing in his eyes.

Morland bustled forward and said, "Just the fellow we wanted to see, Monty. Would you mind taking Debbie home? She ain't feeling well. Something she ate, no doubt."

Montaigne was so shocked at the request that he hardly knew what to say. To be seen escorting Debora would provide fine fuel for the gossipmongers.

"Not Monty, Dick," the duchess said, and whispered something in his ear.

As Dick immediately said, "Witherspoon, then?" Montaigne assumed Debora had alerted him to scandal.

Witherspoon, hoping to win an invitation to the house party at Hastings, agreed with alacrity.

"You'll come along with us then, Monty," Morland said. "Won't take no for an answer. Sissie and Witherspoon came in my rig. He'll take it back to the house. You have your own rig? Excellent. Then you can give Sissie and me a lift. I reserved a large table. A few others will be joining my party."

Morland took Cicely's arm and ushered her out. She cast a questioning look over his shoulder to Montaigne. He didn't want to give Sissie the news of her book in front of the duke, nor did he have much opportunity. Morland kept up a stream of foolish chatter as they drove to the Clarendon. Sissie showed Montaigne her perfume and orchid. She was so impressed at His Grace's lavish treatment that the praise came easily.

"A real orchid! I shall press it and keep it for a memento, along with the lovely perfume bottle."

"Just a little something to please the ladies," he said dismissively. "Debora had the perfume made up from the roses in our garden by a French perfumer. It's called Debora."

He noticed, though, how grateful Cicely was. A fellow liked a little enthusiasm when he went a mile out of his way to please a lady. Debora was never enthusiastic about anything these days. This dinner she was walking away from would bowl Sissie over. Three courses and three removes. Jacquiers was particularly good at *l'oie braisée aux racines glacées*. And his *filets de volaille à l'orléanaise*—why, there wasn't a chef in London could touch him. As for the entremets, a few simple plates of *truffes sous la cendre*, *canards sauvages*, and *petits pains à la duchesse* would do for a start.

At the hotel, Morland casually informed his guests he had had the French chef Jacquiers make them up a bite. "The only place in London one can get a decent French dinner," he mentioned. The "decent French dinner" would cost him four pounds per head, and another guinea per bottle, which was of no more concern to him than the tuppence he might pay for a journal.

His guests were impressed and happy, he was noisy and happy, and the dinner was a great success. Cicely was possibly the happiest person at the table. She hadn't much privacy to discover what had

143

happened at Murray's, but Montaigne found a moment to whisper, "Don't worry. He likes it," and that was enough to make her evening.

At least Murray hadn't hated it. Cicely would have to do some revising over the winter, take out the scene of the pig in the garden—though it was one of her favorites. She had chuckled to herself as she wrote it, remembering Anne chasing after the old sow, Hildie, with the broom. If she worked hard, she could have the manuscript ready for spring.

Made expansive by relief, she lavished praise on the food, although she found it tasted rather strange. She also inquired exhaustively into its contents and preparation, all in the way of research. Morland was delighted to find a fellow gourmet. When Cicely asked if he'd mind if she just jotted down a few notes, he was flattered to death.

Even when dinner was finally over—and it lasted two hours—she still had to wait to hear the whole story from Montaigne. It was arranged that Fairly and Meg would drive Sissie home, while Montaigne was to deliver the slightly inebriated duke home to his duchess.

"I am dead. I shall go straight to bed," Meg announced when they arrived at Berkeley Square. They exchanged good nights with Cicely, and Fairly accompanied Meg abovestairs.

Cicely dallied over the removal of her wrap. She felt it was probably improper to receive Montaigne alone at such an hour, but she knew in her bones he would come. He couldn't be so cruel as to leave her in suspense until the morrow.

The fire in the grate had been banked for the night. It neither flamed nor flared. A sluggish warmth that took the bitter edge off the cold issued from beneath the blanket of coals. Cicely huddled into her shawl. It was ten minutes before she heard the quiet clopping of Montaigne's team in the street. He had his driver set a slow pace to diminish the noise.

He planned to drive by, and if the lights downstairs were extinguished, he would leave and return in the morning. When he saw the light in the saloon, he knew Sissie was waiting for him. A warm glow engulfed him, to be the bearer of good news.

Cicely rose as one in a trance to meet Montaigne as he entered the saloon. "What did he say? Tell me everything," she said, and held her breath until she heard the answer.

Montaigne read the hope and fear in her dark eyes, and his heart swelled with joy at the chore awaiting him.

"He loved it. Sorry I was late at the theater, but once he got his nose into the book, he wouldn't stop reading. I darted home to change while he finished it, then went back for his verdict. Of course he wants to publish it."

Cicely felt a giddiness and a soaring joy such as she had never known possible. She stood stunned to silence for a moment. "Really?" is all she said when she recovered her wits. Then she rushed forward and pitched herself toward Montaigne.

His arms closed around her, holding her tightly against him. A surge of warmth engulfed him as they stood together, her curls tickling his chin, while a faint aroma of flowers wafted around him.

Cicely was startled at his response. She had acted on the spur of the moment, intending only to show her gratitude. She hadn't expected Montaigne to crush her against him in a bear hug and not let go.

145

In fact, his arms began to tighten until Cicely became acutely aware of the hard wall of his chest and his masculine warmth. She wasn't prepared for the way her body responded, either. An unfamiliar thrill lifted the hair on her arms and sent shivers of delightful apprehension down her spine. She suddenly felt awkward, with her arms around his neck.

She glanced up shyly and dropped her arms, but still Montaigne held her loosely around the waist, as if he didn't want to let her go. His dark eyes gazed at her in a strangely intimate, questioning way. The way a man looked at a woman he found attractive . . . The heat began in Cicely's chest and rose to her head, until she felt uncomfortably hot and breathless. She remembered Anne's lecture— she was too old to be doing this with Montaigne.

"Well, aren't you going to let me go?" she asked gruffly.

His expression dwindled to disappointment, then changed to a casual smile so quickly that Cicely wasn't sure she hadn't imagined that brief grimace. "I was hoping for a kiss," Montaigne said, dropping a careless peck on her cheek. Her skin felt as if it had been scalded. Then he released her and gave himself a mental shake.

"I've heard of killing the messenger of bad news," she said, adjusting her shawl. "I didn't know you were supposed to kiss him if he brought good news."

"No doubt it was your throwing yourself into my arms like a hussy that raised my hopes. That is not a complaint, Cicely," he added, smiling. He had never called her Cicely before, except when he was angry. How odd. He had realized she was all grown-up now.

"Tell me what Murray said. Did he really like it?"

They took up a seat in front of the grate.

"I can't imagine why he would lie about it. He spoke of an early release date. Ten thousand copies, in three volumes."

"And I don't have to pay him anything?"

"Au contraire." He mentioned the sum Murray had in mind.

"I shall buy the fur-lined cape for Morland's party," she said. "But did he not complain of the pig in the garden? Sir Giles felt—"

"He particularly enjoyed that scene," Montaigne announced with the greatest satisfaction. That should write finis to Sir Giles. "Its homey humor matched the tone of the rest."

"I can't believe it. I shan't sleep a wink tonight."

"There is the problem of what name to use for the author, since it is fairly well established that you wrote *Chaos*. The two books are so different Murray feels it would lead to confusion in the readers if we tout you as the author of both. I feel a villain for having saddled you with authorship of the inferior novel, making it impossible—well, difficult at least—to claim the honor of your own."

"I don't care about that," she said. "My family and close friends will know I wrote it. They're the only ones who matter to me. It can be by another anonymous lady. A provincial lady. Or we can just make up a name. Aunt Ethel, perhaps," she said, laughing.

"Chaos is not a book that will last. After a few years, and a few more volumes from your pen, folks will forget about Eugenie, and you can claim full honors for *Georgiana. Chaos* will be chalked up to your first, youthful effort."

"I'm really not at all concerned about that."

"Well, it has been bothering *me*. I'm relieved you take it so lightly. We should celebrate, Cicely. Shall I ask the butler for a bottle of Fairly's champagne?"

Cicely felt again that strange discomfort she had felt when Montaigne held her in his arms. It was the way he studied her, with a pensive, penetrating gaze, as if he were looking at some creature he hadn't seen before. It left her ill at ease.

"I'm already floating on Morland's champagne," she said. "Did you ever sit down to such a feast before?"

"Yes, at Carlton House. I never before heard a lady lavish so much praise, however."

"I wanted to find out a little about it—for my research, you know. It was all so beautiful and tasted so funny. It was that French chef who was to blame."

Blame! His lips quirked in a smile. What would Morland say if he heard that? "Jacquiers is top of the trees. He cooked for Louis the Eighteenth before coming to England."

"No wonder Louis was fat as a flawn. Everything so rich, and the desserts all awash in sour cream."

"It was liqueurs that gave the cream that taste."

"That's right. Dick told me." She soon returned to the more interesting topic. "What about revisions? And a contract. Shall I call on Murray?"

"He'll call here tomorrow morning, since you're going out with Witherspoon in the afternoon."

"I'd forgotten all about it. Witherspoon seems nice," she said, thinking back to the earlier part of the evening.

"Our touring of London will have to wait another day. I'll be in touch with Meg to see what is on for

148

the evening. And now, I expect I should leave, since it is three A.M."

"Is it really? I don't feel a bit sleepy."

"London is seducing you into bad habits."

"I shall be quite spoiled when I return to Elmdale. I must write to Anne before I go to bed. She'll be so excited for me."

"Send her my regards. And now I must be off."

She accompanied him to the door. "Did you manage to eat your humble pie, or were you too busy gourmandizing on the French fare?"

"I didn't get around to it. I'll send Morland a note tomorrow."

Montaigne waved the butler away when he came to open the door. He wanted a last moment alone with Cicely. But once the door was open, an arctic blast of air made lingering impossible.

"Thank you, Monty," she said, reaching for his hand.

He lifted her outstretched hand and brushed a light kiss on her fingers. "*À demain,*" he said and left.

Despite the cold breeze, Cicely stood a moment, watching as Montaigne left. He had never kissed her hand before. What had come over him? She decided it was all part and parcel of London manners. Now that Cicely was becoming "seduced" by London, he was treating her like a London lady. That's all it meant. It would be foolish to go thinking it meant anything more.

Chapter Fifteen

Mr. Murray called on Cicely early in the morning to arrange the details of her contract. He was enthusiastic about her work. Together they discussed a few modest changes, which she undertook to make. The book was to be published in the new year.

After such a start to her day, the rest of the morning was an anticlimax. The visit to Bedlam was never intended as a pleasure jaunt, but it was made extremely uncomfortable by the company of the Duke of Morland. Witherspoon had told Debora of the outing, she had told the duke, and he had invited himself along, using the ploy that his presence would insure good treatment, as indeed it did. They were greeted most cordially and given a guided tour of the premises.

Cicely could not think Morland's pointing and gawping and laughing at misfortune was pleasant, even for lunatics. Their case was so miserable she felt ill. The worst ones were locked up in cells, where they ranted and raved, pounded the walls, and pulled their hair. The less violent inmates sat around the place on benches or the floor, looking so desolate she wanted to cry. The ragged clothes, the clotted hair, the fetid air, the indifference of the guards, and the futility of it all were enough to drive a sane person to madness.

"If they wasn't mad when they went in, they soon would be," Morland said, with a rare insight, when they left. "Can't imagine why you wanted to see 'em, Sissie. The stuff of nightmares. Let us stroll along Bond Street to clear our palates."

Witherspoon had received his invitation to Hastings and was eager to oblige His Grace. Cicely was becoming a little known in London. A few heads turned to see her on the strut with the duke. Morland insisted on buying her a memento of the trip to Bedlam. She had great difficulty controlling his generosity. He felt a little diamond brooch was just the ticket. Cicely finally agreed to accept a fan made of ivory slats ingeniously painted to show the Parthenon when closed; when opened, its silk expansion showed a peacock in full display.

"It will always remind me of you," she said with unsteady lips, as her eyes flickered over the peacock elaboration of his toilette. Then she quickly closed the fan, lest he take offense.

"It does look a little like Hastings," he said, smiling at the picture of the Parthenon.

As he had taken a fancy to the brooch, he bought it as well, saying it was for Debora. His intention was to force it on Cicely at some later date. He imagined it was Witherspoon's presence that made her so reluctant to take the trinket.

The duke dropped Witherspoon off at the Albany and drove Cicely back to Berkeley Square, where he invited himself in to say good day to the Fairlys, in hopes of receiving an invitation to lunch. Fairly was out, but Meg had just returned from shopping. Morland was desolate to learn Cicely was busy that afternoon. She had uphill work convincing him he could not accompany her to her meeting with Palin and Moore. "It is a business meeting," she insisted.

"Gad, what a bluestocking you are, Sissie! This evening, then," he said. "What are you and Fairly doing, Meg?"

"Nothing in particular. Perhaps a concert."

"Then you'll dine with us," he said. "Won't take no for an answer. Deb will love to have you. She is blue as megrims lately. Don't know what ails her. She does nothing but lie in her bed, complaining. I'll have some entertainers from Drury Lane in to serenade us afterward. Or perhaps a little dance."

Cicely, who had had quite sufficient of His Grace's company, said, "Montaigne mentioned dropping by to do something this evening, Meg."

"Excellent! Bring him along," the duke said. "P'raps he can cheer Deb up. Blue-deviled lately, poor girl."

"I cannot answer for him," she said.

"Make him come. Don't take no for an answer."

Morland soon left to arrange the dinner and evening's entertainment. He decided that dancing was better than a musical evening after all. Waltzing would provide a good chance to get Cicely in his arms. Dashed pretty chit, and lively. Always something pleasant to say. He'd give her the little brooch that evening.

The meeting with Palin and Moore went off with no difficulty. Meg decided that Sissie shouldn't go alone and made Fairly accompany her. As the meeting occurred at Covent Garden, he was well entertained by the actresses, who were in rehearsal for a new production.

Montaigne, busy at the House, didn't call on the

Fairlys that afternoon. Cicely wrote him a note directed to his home, telling him he was invited to the Morlands for dinner and entertainment after. She had no reply. Montaigne didn't receive the note until he returned home at six-thirty, at which time he wrote to the duchess apologizing for the tardiness of his reply, declining the dinner invitation, but saying he would drop in later for the entertainment.

It was another elaborate evening. Two dozen guests had been scraped together at the last minute. The French chef had been busy with his minions, creating a menu fit for Lucullus. An orchestra was hired. Morland had spent some time in his library searching out titles that might make an excuse to lure Cicely into that room for a little flirtation. No harm in it. He was a gentleman, and she wasn't a deb, after all. A dashed bluestocking. Up to every rig and racket in town.

Cicely wore again the rose gown with Anne's diamonds. As a courtesy to the duke, she brought along the peacock fan. The mansion on Grosvenor Square was as elaborate and overadorned as she expected. From the exterior, it resembled St. Paul's, with a huge dome on top. Inside, a bevy of liveried footmen and maids in frilled aprons scuttled about the vast marble expanse of hallway. Three huge half-circle arches of green Galway marble led into the saloon. They were surrounded by dark, soaring walls of carved teak. Numberless lamps gleamed on red brocade and enough gilt to furnish a palace. And with all its finery, the house was ugly as sin. Nothing matched or harmonized with anything else. The host and hostess were dwarfed by the thronelike chairs they sat in.

The first of Morland's dinners had been an interesting novelty. During the second, Cicely became bored. There was no intelligent conversation but only an endless round of gossip and loud laughter. The food was too rich, there was too much of it, and too much wine. By the time the meal was over, Cicely felt stifled. She longed to go out for a long walk in the fresh air, but it was impossible. The gentlemen remained behind for port until nearly ten o'clock. Cicely found herself looking to the arches, wishing Montaigne would come. Perhaps he wasn't coming. She feared the duke would make a dash for her when the gentlemen joined the ladies and took the precaution of sitting with Debora.

The duchess was a little stiff with her. "Witherspoon tells me Dickie took you to Bedlam this afternoon," she said.

"His Grace decided to accompany Mr. Witherspoon and myself. We had planned the outing a few days ago," Cicely replied, hoping to make clear the duke's coming was none of her doing. Thinking to ingratiate Debora, she asked, "Did you like the diamond brooch he bought you?"

Debora stared at her with bright curiosity in her amethyst eyes. "He didn't buy me a brooch," she said.

"Oh, dear! I'm sorry! No doubt it was to be a surprise. I shouldn't have spoken."

"No doubt," Debora said in icy accents. Then she rose and went to sit with Lady Varley.

When the gentlemen finally came, the duke headed straight for Cicely. She was uncomfortably aware of those violet eyes staring at her accusingly from across the room.

"It is to be a waltzing party," he said. "Just an informal little do. No need to bother with cotillions and minuets. We shall have the first waltz, Sissie."

"I think you should have the first set with your wife," she said.

He laughed merrily. "Deb wouldn't thank me for that. She'll stand up with young Weatherspoon, her new flirt. Not the thing for a gentleman to hang on his wife's skirt tails, Sis. Look a dashed quiz. We shall have the first set." He had spent the afternoon in Witherspoon's company but hadn't bothered to learn his name.

As Fairly was leading some lady other than Meg to the ballroom, Cicely assumed this was another London custom and went along with Morland. He was an exuberant waltzer, if not a particularly good one. He swooped and whirled and cavorted about the ballroom, arms driving up and down like a pump handle, coattails flying. Fortunately the room was large and the dancers few, so that he didn't capsize anyone.

When Montaigne stepped in at ten-thirty, the first thing he saw was Morland swooping about like an inebriated swallow, while Cicely held on for dear life. When she looked up and spotted Montaigne, she made a pleading face. His bad humor faded to be replaced by amusement. He would let her suffer! And besides, it would look odd for him to cut in. As soon as the set ended, he went to her rescue.

"Ah, Monty!" Morland said. "What kept you? You missed a dandy dinner. The *côtelettes de mouton à la française* were rather special, if I do say so myself, eh, Sissie? I daresay you was sunk to one of those wretched beefsteaks at your club."

Morland didn't wait for a reply but rattled on with other features of the menu until the music resumed, and Montaigne swept Cicely into his arms.

Chapter Sixteen

"I see I was greatly missed by Morland. Did *you* miss me?" he asked, glinting a curiously intimate smile at her.

"Wretchedly! I am beginning to have grave doubts about this house party at Hastings. It is to last nearly a week. I shan't be able to get into my gowns by the time it is over."

Montaigne was in good spirits to hear the duke's overpowering style was beginning to pall on Cicely. "You can hide your avoirdupois under a fur-lined pelisse," he said playfully.

"I wish I had it now, and I'd go out for a walk. I know how a Strasbourg goose feels."

Montaigne's easy glide about the floor was a pleasant change from Morland's erratic flight. His conversation was also a relief from the inanity that had preceded it. He asked how Cicely's busy day had gone. He heard a sensible account of her two working visits and an amusing recital of the trip to Bedlam. Yet he was aware of the genuine concern lurking beneath her tale of Morland's antics at Bedlam.

He was especially gratified when Cicely asked him what he had been doing at Whitehall. Ladies didn't usually take any interest in politics. He waited until the set was over, then led her to the refreshment parlor and told her of the latest political imbroglio.

"That loose screw, Czar Alexander of Russia, has fallen prey to a mystic, Madame Krüdener, and is trying to bind Europe in a Holy Alliance. It is more a profession of faith than a political document. Something to the effect that the nations have no other sovereign but God. It recommends that the people fortify themselves to practice the duties Christianity enjoins on them. Meaningless verbiage that wouldn't stand up a minute once a shot was fired. The simpleminded king of Prussia and others are going along with it.

"Since our king is hors de combat, the matter has fallen into Prinny's incapable hands. Our constitutional government prevents him from committing England to such an alliance without the consent of Parliament—thank God. We are hoping the thing does go to Parliament. We would have a heyday with it, but of course that wily devil Castlereagh will wiggle out of it somehow. Perhaps have Prinny write a personal letter of approval that falls short of a formal agreement."

"Is that the way you spend your days? Here I pictured you making sensible laws for our welfare."

"No, no. I, too, spent the day at Bedlam. It's good comic relief, and at least it don't cost anything. No new taxes will be required in a world without armies."

"I'm sure you politicians will find some new excuse to gouge us. More churches, perhaps. Have you spoken to Morland about that humble pie?"

"Not yet. That's the other reason I am here."

"The other reason? What is the main reason?"

158

He studied her over the rim of his glass. His dark eyes gleamed flirtatiously. "Hmmm," he murmured. "I must be slipping. Do you really have to ask, Cicely?"

"One gallant an evening is quite enough for me. Don't you start flirting and pretending you like me, too. If you want to be sure of that invitation, speak to the duchess. I doubt she'll refuse you."

"Flirting?" he asked, feigning offense. "A fine way to talk to an M.P. who has wasted—spent—hours arguing the Holy Alliance. A little respect for your elders, miss. Let a lady sell a book and she sets up as the equal of an M.P. You're not the only person with a contract from Murray in your pocket."

"No, but I am the only one with a contract from Lord Montaigne," she retorted. "You'd best watch your step with me, Master Jackanapes."

"You don't mean to let me forget it for a moment," he said in jest. Then, more seriously, "Perhaps it is time to normalize relations with Debora. I've been avoiding her as much as possible, but I can hardly do so for the better part of a week at Hastings. I'll see her now and be back *tout de suite*."

Morland was on the alert for Sissie. When he saw Montaigne enter the ballroom alone, he went off after her and found her in the refreshment parlor, finishing her wine.

"Ah, Sissie. Just the girl I was looking for. I have a book in my library I must show you. Just the sort of thing a bluestocking like yourself would appreciate."

"I don't consider myself a bluestocking," she replied, but as it was a foregone conclusion the duke wouldn't take no for an answer, Cicely went to the library. It was better than waltzing with him again.

She was dismayed to see the library was empty. Like all the chambers, it was huge and decorated to excess. It held more statuary and Roman vases than books, though there was one wall of books in burgundy leather with gold embossing. Their perfect arrangement on the shelves suggested they were untouched by anything but a goose-wing duster. As Morland left the double doors to the hallway open, Cicely assumed that he did actually have a book in mind to show her.

The main point of the visit was to give her the brooch, but as she was acting stiffish, Morland went to the bookshelves, scanning for a title that might amuse Cicely. The title *Ars amatoria*, by Ovid, caught his eye. The high seriousness of a Horace, the *Bucolics* and *Georgics* of a Virgil were not for him. If a fellow had to study Latin, Ovid was the thing to study.

"Here it is," he said, opening the book at random. He began to read in Latin, pacing back and forth and imagining he was on a stage, with hundreds of admirers. The Latin might as well have been Greek or Sanskrit, for all it meant to Cicely—or Morland, for that matter. She sat and let him read, as it kept him out of mischief and gave her a moment to collect her thoughts. She knew the Fairlys would stay until two or three in the morning, but perhaps Montaigne would leave earlier and give her a drive home. She only had to interrupt her scheming from time to time to clap or say, "That was charming, Dick."

Morland enjoyed the performance but eventually realized he could be spending this private moment more profitably. He sat down beside Cicely and closed the book. "But enough of that," he said. "You know why I invited you here."

"It was very enjoyable. Thank you. And now we ought to join the others." She rose.

Morland rose and grasped her fingers. His other hand went into his pocket. Palming the diamond brooch, he lifted his hand to her bodice to attach it to her gown.

Cicely leaped in alarm when she felt Morland's hand on her breast. "What are you doing?" she exclaimed, brushing it away.

"Don't be shy, Sissie. We're alone. No one need know."

"Know what? What are you talking about?" She looked down and saw the sparkle of diamonds on her gown.

She lifted her hand and unfastened the brooch. Morland caught her fingers, pressing his hand against hers on her breast. His other arm went around her waist. Giving him the slap he deserved was difficult with her left hand, especially when they stood in such close proximity. The best she could manage was to give his nose a sharp pinch. He squealed, then stepped back.

Cicely thought, for a moment, that she must have really hurt him. Morland stared, turning from pink to rose. "Debora!" he cried in a high, breathless voice.

From the doorway where she stood, Debora had spotted the diamond brooch. Her violet eyes darkened to deepest purple, just as in *Chaos Is Come Again* when Eugenie mistakenly believed Ravencroft had betrayed her. Their shade was made more noticeable by her frozen, white face. "Am I interrupting you? So sorry," she said in glacial accents

161

only slightly marred by a hiccup of tears, and stalked from the room.

Morland took a step after her and came up against the wall of Montaigne's chest in the doorway. "What the hell's going on?" Montaigne demanded in a voice like thunder.

"Let me go! Debora is unwell," Morland said and fled.

Montaigne directed his anger at Cicely. "May I know the meaning of this?" he asked, advancing stiffly toward her.

"If you can figure it out, I wish you will tell me."

"I left you for a moment in the refreshment parlor. When I returned with Debora, you weren't there. The servants said you and Morland had come here—alone."

"He said he wanted to show me some book. He was reading to me, then he suddenly tried to give me this diamond brooch." She looked down and saw the brooch was gone. Morland had managed to get hold of it when he spotted Debora. Or perhaps it had fallen off. Cicely remembered unpinning it. A quick search showed her it wasn't on the floor. "He must have taken it before he left."

She explained about the shopping trip after the visit to Bedlam and the brooch supposedly bought for Debora. "Surely he cannot think I would accept diamonds from him!" she said indignantly.

They sat on the sofa. Montaigne crossed his legs and sighed, satisfied with her explanation. "Diamonds mean no more to Morland than that little fan," he said, nodding at the fan on the sofa.

She threw it across the room in disgust. "Idiot!" she scowled. "There is one good thing about it. I

162

really cannot be expected to go to Hastings after this. Debora probably thinks I was encouraging him."

"And just when I have been at some pains to get my invitation reinstated."

"I suppose I shall have to face Debora sooner or later and explain. Well, invent some story to account for her seeing that brooch on me."

"As your forte is fiction, that should be simple. He was asking your opinion of it as a gift for Debora, perhaps?"

"She might believe that. I already let slip that he bought it for her. Still, it will be embarrassing. I'll get it over with now and leave." She looked a question at him. "That is, if you—Or I could borrow Fairly's carriage. He and Meg will stay till the last dog is hung."

"Especially with such an enticing new *on dit* to chew over. He didn't try to molest you?"

"I trust you mean kiss me? No, he didn't. I daresay he expected a kiss in gratitude for the brooch, the fool. I should have slapped his face. The best I could do was pinch his nose."

Montaigne, biting back a smile, picked up the book. "Is this what he was reading to you?" he asked.

"Yes, what is it?"

"Loosely translated, *Excerpts from the Roman Light-Skirts' Handbook.*"

"Is *that* what it is!" she exclaimed angrily. "Shocking! He read it in Latin, you see. I hadn't a notion what any of it meant. He probably hadn't, either. He just enjoyed strutting about, declaiming, pretending he was Kean."

"Pretending?"

"Kean, the actor, I meant."

"Ah. Shall I ask Debora to come in here for a moment?"

"Would you mind?"

Montaigne's eyes glittered dangerously. "Not at all. It will give me the opportunity for a private word with His Grace."

He left but returned a moment later, wearing a frustrated expression. "The Morlands have retired for the evening and don't wish to be disturbed. Typical! A house full of guests, and the hosts go to bed. Yahoos!" Cicely laughed. "Come. I'll take you home."

As no serious harm had come to Cicely, Montaigne was just as glad the contretemps had occurred. It alerted her to the dangers adrift for a greenhorn in London and wrote finis to the Hastings party.

"Not all the gentlemen are so harmless as Morland," he explained as they drove through the darkness. A light fog had settled in. The stark outline of nude branches formed a tracery above in the mist.

"Even a Morland could make mincemeat of a lady's reputation," she said. "I definitely shan't go to Hastings, even if Debora asks me. I cannot think she will after tonight."

"Debora is peculiarly forgiving. Morland's tried his stunts with most of their female friends. Last year it was Lord Harelton's young wife. A diamond bracelet."

"What did she do?" Cicely asked, staring in astonishment.

"Kept it," he said with a *tsk* of disgust.

"Did she—"

"No, she didn't. She's not that bad. Nor did Morland expect her to. Until a lady has given her husband a son or two, she is expected to limit her favors to him. A man likes to know his heir is his own flesh and blood."

"Gracious! They even have rules about adultery! Very practical, of course, but when sin is regulated, it gives it the air of being acceptable."

"An astute observation."

When the carriage drew up in front of Fairly's mansion, Montaigne said, "May I come in for a moment, or have you had enough of gentlemen imposing their presence on you for one evening? I promise I have no diamonds up my sleeve."

"What I would really like is to go for a little walk. It was so hot and stuffy at the Morlands', and the food was so rich I felt nearly ill. We needn't go far. You won't want to leave your team standing long."

Montaigne took Cicely's elbow and they walked down the street with the fog caressing their cheeks. It was warm for December. Patches of light from saloon windows cast hazy puddles of orange into the mist.

"Now that we won't be going to Hastings, will you return to Elmdale on the tenth or remain in London?" he asked.

"Perhaps split the difference. The extra few days will give me time for a little more sightseeing. But why do you say *we* won't be going? There is no reason for you to withdraw."

Montaigne glared. "Just like a lady! I was only going to keep you out of trouble. I despise that sort of do. Too much drinking and gambling and gossiping and flirting. There won't be a sensible word spoken. I don't know how Meg can abide it. I shall call off."

"Where will you spend Christmas?" she asked.

They reached the end of the block and turned around to retrace their steps. "Do you think your papa would allow you to come to London for the Christmas pantomime? Along with Anne and himself, I mean. It seems a shame for you to miss your moment of glory."

"I know Anne would love it. So would I, but Papa—I'm not sure. We always spend Christmas at home. He would be uncomfortable at a hotel, and I can hardly impose the family on Meg."

"I meant as my guests," he said.

"I wasn't hinting," she said, embarrassed.

"I am aware of that. You're not a hinter. When you want something, you say it. It is one of the things I admire about you."

Cicely grew flustered at this unexpected shower of compliments. She concluded Montaigne was trying to repay her for posing as the author of his book and keeping quiet about it. She stopped walking and stared at him.

"That is extraordinarily generous of you, Montaigne."

He batted this notion away with a flick of his fingers. "The first presentation of the pantomime is on the twenty-third. Your folks could come early, say the twentieth. If your papa is quite bent on Christmas at home, you could leave on the twenty-fourth to be home by Christmas Eve."

A smile trembled on her lips. "I know Anne would love it," she said again.

"And you? Would you like it, Sissie?"

"Oh yes. It would be beyond anything great. I have been writing to Anne. It would be so nice if she were here, someone to share all the ton's foolishness with, you know. You're the only one I can talk to, and you already know all their doings."

"I see them in a new light, through your eyes," he said, gazing down at her. "The eyes of innocence."

"My eyes have been opened since coming to London, though."

Montaigne lifted his hands and cupped Cicely's face in his warm palms. One hand slid down to her chin and tilted her face up to his. He gazed at her for a long moment in silence, then placed a light, fleeting kiss on her lips.

When he spoke, his voice was gentle. "Don't change too much. I like you the way you are."

Cicely just gazed at him silently. She couldn't think of anything to say. The breath seemed to have caught in her throat. Montaigne took her elbow again and led her to the door of Fairly's house.

"Can we begin our tour of London tomorrow?" he asked. "In the afternoon for choice. I shall wage war on the Holy Alliance in the morning."

"And I shall make a few changes to *Georgiana*. Afternoon will be fine. Thank you, Montaigne, for—everything."

"It has been my pleasure."

He tipped his hat and returned to his carriage. Cicely went inside and up to her room. It seemed strange, almost incredible, that Montaigne could have remained so sane in wicked London. He wasn't as rich as Morland, but he was rich enough to indulge in any vice. And, as far as she knew, he ignored them all. He had chosen his bride poorly, and Cicely was glad Debora had refused him. Montaigne required a sensible wife, someone who would encourage him in his work. Someone like—

But that was going a good deal too far. He was

just being polite and thoughtful, wanting to invite Papa and Anne to London. Papa would never consider such a thing. Cicely didn't even plan to ask him. But she was sorry to have to miss seeing her own pantomime.

Chapter Seventeen

Cicely worked on *Georgiana* in the morning, and in the afternoon Montaigne arrived to begin her tours of London. The weather had worsened. The wind was bitterly chill, but in Montaigne's well-sprung carriage with a fur rug over their lap, a thermos of coffee, and warm bricks at their feet, they were as cozy as mice in malt. First he drove her through the prestigious West End, where the wealthy had their mansions, each marked off with iron railings. Some of the windows were boarded and the brass door-knockers removed, indicating the owners were away for the winter. To emphasize the difference, he next drove her through the squalid desolation of Long Acre.

The afternoons were so short in the early part of December, that Montaigne came even earlier the following afternoon. Over the next days, Cicely saw Billingsgate and an art exhibition at Somerset House, hospitals and poorhouses, Carlton House and gin houses (from the outside) and the theater district, ending the last afternoon at the Ladies' Gallery of the House of Parliament to hear a bill being debated on the final day before Christmas recess, when the House was even rowdier than usual.

"I had thought it impossible anything could be

worse than Seven Dials or Bedlam," Cicely said. "I see I was mistaken. I have never been more disgusted in my life than to see Members of Parliament behaving like rowdy schoolboys. Why do they not let the speaker speak? Three-quarters of the seats were empty, and any who *were* there were stamping their feet, uttering catcalls, and throwing paper balls across to the other side of the House."

"The rowdyism is an added difficulty, certainly," Montaigne replied mildly. "And makes it dashed difficult to sleep during the duller speeches, too."

In the evenings, they went out to plays or routs or concerts, usually with the Fairlys and a few other couples. Montaigne broached the matter of Anne and Mr. Caldwell's coming to London for the pantomime again, and again was told that there was no point in suggesting it. Papa would never agree.

The duke called often at Berkeley Square; Coddle had standing instructions to inform him Miss Caldwell was not at home. Cicely had written her note to the duchess, who had not seen fit to reply. On the fourth morning, Cicely was surprised to hear that Debora planned to call on Lady Fairly at eleven o'clock.

"I would like a word with her in private, Meg. Would you mind delaying your arrival in the saloon?"

"I always like to make a grand entrance," Meg said. "But what do you want with Debora? I thought you two were on the outs."

"I want to find out why she didn't answer my note. I apologized for that evening at their house and told her I would not be going to Hastings."

"*You* apologized! Ninnyhammer! It is Dickie who should apologize to you. Shocking, the way he carries on. Perhaps Deb is in a snit because you canceled the visit to Hastings."

When the duchess, resplendent in feathers and furs, was shown into the saloon that morning, she appeared disconcerted to be confronted with Cicely.

"Good day, Miss Cicely," she said coolly. "I hope I find you well?"

"Fine, thank you, Duchess," Cicely replied in similar accents. It had been her intention to call Debora to account, but when she saw the girl looking so pale and drawn, she hadn't the heart for it. Despite the elegance of a sable-lined cape with a lovely fox trim, Debora looked positively ill. The smudges beneath her eyes were nearly as violet as the eyes themselves.

Debora was seated. She made a business of removing her gloves, to avoid looking at Cicely. Eventually she said, "I'm sorry you won't be able to join us at Hastings."

"I should think you'd be relieved," Cicely said with her customary frankness.

Debora was so shocked to hear the truth that she was momentarily stunned into silence. "Indeed I am very sorry," she repeated.

"Let us not waste time in fustian. We have only a moment to talk. I'm sorry if I have inadvertently caused you dismay. Your husband was not giving me that diamond brooch, Debora. You misjudge me if you think I would accept such a gift from a gentleman."

"I know it," Debora said. "It's not your fault. He is always chasing after some woman. If it's not you, it will be someone else. He doesn't mean anything by it."

"Why do you put up with it?"

171

"Because I love him." Her bottom lip began to tremble, and she added in a low voice, "I'm afraid of losing him, and I am enceinte." Then she burst into a fit of moist tears.

"Enceinte! Does the duke know?"

Debora drew out a dainty lace-edged handkerchief and sniffled into it. "I haven't told him. The truth is, Dick and I don't see much of each other these days. He is very busy," she added in a pathetic attempt to whitewash her gallivanting husband.

"I see." Cicely sat a moment, digesting this state of affairs. Her heart went out to Debora in her sorrow. She was every bit as witless as Eugenie Beaureport. Something must be done, and before long Cicely had come up with a plan.

By the time Meg made her grand entrance, the duchess's violet eyes were not only dry but sparkling with mischief. Meg had to be taken into confidence, as she was to be involved in the plan's success. Her job was to keep Fairly out of the house that afternoon. Debora and Meg were off to rifle the shops. When the duke arrived an hour later, he was told that Miss Cicely was out but would be home at three.

"Tell Miss Cicely I shall pop 'round at three, then. There's a good fellow."

Cicely dashed a note off to Montaigne, canceling her drive with him. To insure that he didn't come pouncing in to destroy her plan, she told him she had a meeting with Mr. Moore that afternoon. She would explain the matter to him that evening. She spent the remainder of her morning finishing her revisions to *Georgiana* and sent the manuscript off to Mr. Murray via a footman.

After lunch, Meg took Fairly to view the latest exhibition at Somerset House. The duke arrived at three on the dot, carrying a monstrous bouquet of flowers. To his delight, he found Cicely alone in the saloon. She greeted him with a warm smile and indicated a seat beside her on the sofa in front of the blazing grate. She called the butler.

"Will you please put these flowers in water, Coddle. And if anyone calls, I am not at home. You may close the door after you."

Morland could scarcely believe his ears. He hadn't expected such cooperation from Cicely. In fact, he was a little disconcerted at it. Pretty fast for an unmarried lady! He soon came to terms with the new situation, however—bluestocking, up to all the rigs—and sat beside her on the sofa.

"Now what is this nonsense of your not coming to Hastings, Sissie? Do come. It won't be any fun without you. Dash it, I only arranged the do to get to know you better."

"We can get to know each better here," she said leadingly. "After that embarrassing episode with the diamond brooch, I didn't think the duchess would want me to go."

"Much difference it will make to her," he pouted. "She'll probably take to her bed the minute we reach Hastings."

"Is she ill?"

"She's turning into a chronic invalid. That's what it is. Be buying shawls and ordering possets and catlap, next thing you know. Of course I still love her," he added, lest Cicely take the notion he was contemplating divorce, or some such thing. He had no desire to be cut off from Society by a divorce.

"She is very beautiful."

"Aye, she was. *Is!* But she don't have your life,

173

Sissie. You are always up to something exciting. Dashing off books and plays and I don't know what all. I haven't been able to see you all week."

"You are seeing me now," she pointed out.

He took the hint and moved closer. "I'm very angry with you," he said, shaking a finger in mock scolding.

"Why, what have I done to displease you?"

"You know perfectly well, minx. That diamond brooch. Rubbishy trinket, and you wouldn't accept it. I'd like to shower you with diamonds."

Cicely batted her lashes shamelessly. "It is very improper of you to say that to me. Gentlemen only give diamonds to their *chères amies*." Her straining ears heard the approach of a carriage in the roadway. Debora was right on time.

The duke uttered an uncomfortable laugh. "Good God! Is that what you thought I was up to! Nothing of the sort. You ain't even married. I just wanted us to be good friends." As she obviously suspected him of being a much more dashing fellow than he was, he felt he ought to make some token of living up to her expectations. "Mind you, I am tempted."

She smiled encouragingly as the echo of the front door quietly opening came to her ears. "That would be very naughty, Dickie."

"Just one little kiss. No harm in that. Won't take no for an answer."

He lunged at her and got his hands on her shoulders. He was leaning awkwardly forward, trying to apply his lips to hers, when the saloon door opened and the duchess stepped in.

Morland froze, his hands on Cicely's shoulders. Cicely clutched onto his waist, in case he tried to get away. "Debora!" he gasped. Debora advanced, purple eyes flashing fire. "It's not what you think! We were just—practicing."

Her chin rose and she spoke with commendable disdain. "You hardly need practice at seduction, Duke! If you haven't mastered the art during all the years you have been working at it, you are beyond hope. I shall be leaving for my father's estate today. Your lawyer may contact him there about arrangements for our separation."

She turned to sweep from the room in a fine fling of sable. There wasn't a sign of a tear in those violet eyes that watered up so easily. The duke was horrified. To add to Morland's consternation, Debora ran smack into Montaigne in the doorway. He stood blocking her exit like a jailer, a most murderous fire in his eye. The duke uttered a strangled gasp and stared helplessly, like a rabbit hypnotized by a weasel.

Chapter Eighteen

The duke disentangled himself from Cicely's arms and leaped to his feet.

"It ain't what you think, neither of you!" he said. "Tell them, Miss Cicely."

"I was just telling Dickie it would be most improper of him to shower me with diamonds as he wants to," she said with an innocent smile.

Montaigne pounced forward, his hands already balled into fists. He didn't usually strike a gentleman smaller than himself, but his temper was so hot that he didn't hesitate a moment to land the duke a facer. Debora gave one wince as the sound of flesh striking flesh hung on the air, and the duke crumpled to the sofa. Blood began to ooze from his nose. Cicely handed him her handkerchief. She didn't want to destroy Meg's nice satin striped sofa. The duke was fully conscious—and fully aware that flat on his back was the safest place for him to remain. He moaned, holding the linen to his nose, thinking Debora might come to his aid.

"Well done, Monty!" the duchess declared and flounced from the room.

"Debbie! Wait! I say!" The duke struggled to his feet and slunk out the door. Cicely had to suppress an eruption of laughter. Morland's awkward gait, knees bent, gave him the air of a monkey as he peered fearfully over his shoulder to see if Montaigne was coming after him.

Only then did Cicely look to Montaigne. He stood, arms akimbo, glancing at her with an expression very similar to that he'd worn just before striking the duke.

"What is the meaning of this?" he demanded.

Instead of answering, Cicely rushed to the window to look out and see if Debora got into the carriage with the duke or went to her own rig. The couple stood on the street, arguing. The duke's hands rose in silent supplication. The duchess tossed her head in rebuke. Cicely wished she could hear them.

"Cicely, I'm speaking to you!" Montaigne roared.

"I am not deaf, Montaigne. Do be quiet," she called over her shoulder.

His patience broke, and he lit into a tirade. "Have you lost the use of whatever wits you possess? Carrying on like a light-skirt! I might have known when I brought you here! I warned you against this sort of carry-on. You've been encouraging that mawworm behind my back."

"Well of course I have, stoopid!" she said, just glancing at him. She looked again to the street, where Debora was tossing her head petulantly. But she let the duke put his arm around her. Excellent!

Montaigne's wrath was further aggravated by this cavalier response to his rant. "You have the bold-faced gall to admit it! Carrying on with a married man. Encouraging him to give you diamonds."

"No, trying to discourage him, actually."

He strode to the window, clamped his hands on Cicely's shoulders and turned her around to face him. His angry face, flushed with fury, loomed over hers. She could hear his heavy breaths, feel their warm rush on her face. Montaigne's eyes glowed like live coals. It was very gratifying, but Cicely could not stop to appreciate it. Glancing over his shoulder, she saw the duke staring in disbelieve at Debora's stomach area. She had told him that she was enceinte, then. Ah, good! Dickie was kissing her. Oh, dear. Cicely feared the violet eyes were watering up again. Morland was daubing at them with Debora's handkerchief. The duchess was led into the duke's splendid carriage with the strawberry leaves on the door with all the care afforded to an invalid queen. A dazzling smile settled on Cicely's face.

"Sorry. What were you saying, Monty?" she asked calmly.

He quelled the urge to strangle her and said, "Did you accept diamonds from him?"

"Of course not! I told him it would be quite improper!"

"You let him put his arms around you."

"Well of course I did."

Montaigne's jaws tightened. He growled through his teeth, "I'll challenge the bastard to a duel."

"How can he be a bastard? You told me there are strict rules about such things."

"Much that would matter to him—or you!"

"Surely you are confused, Montaigne. It would be his mama who had misbehaved, would it not?"

"This is not a joking matter, Cicely. Have you any notion of what will happen to your reputation when this scandal gets about? You'll be ruined."

She walked to the sofa, sat down, and began tidying her skirt unconcernedly. "Do you seriously believe the duke will spread this particular piece of gossip? It makes him look an ass."

"Their separation can hardly be kept secret. Debora will certainly broadcast the tale."

"Oh no. She has agreed not to say a word. It was all to be kept *en famille*—until you came along," she added with a scowl. "What are you doing here? I told you I was busy."

"You told me you had a meeting with Moore."

"Well, I had to make some excuse."

"Lying, on top of the rest! I don't understand you, Cicely. London has totally corrupted you."

"I am not made of such stern stuff as you, Montaigne." Then she laughed. "Don't be such a clunch. It was all arranged."

Montaigne's nostrils thinned to slits. "An assignation? How did you get rid of Meg and Fairly?"

"Meg has taken Fairly to Somerset House, but they should be back soon."

His outrage soared. "You admit you schemed to meet Morland alone?"

"Of course I did. There was no counting on him to misbehave if there were other people present." Her lips moved unsteadily, for she was perfectly aware of Montaigne's confusion and consternation. He would not be so furious if he didn't care for her more than just a little. When he continued glaring, Cicely laughed aloud.

Montaigne began to understand there was more to the debauch he had just observed than he realized. The violent upheaval in his chest eased noticeably.

"Perhaps you could control your hysteria long enough to explain this unsavory affair to me?" he said grimly.

"Well, I shall try, but it was really very funny when you came pouncing in and drew Dick's cork. We hadn't anticipated that. Did you hear Debora? 'Well done, Monty!' she said."

"This scheme was engineered by you ladies, I take it?"

"Yes, to teach Dickie a lesson. He has been ignoring Debora quite shamefully, carrying on with any lady who will give him the time of day—and in her condition. She is enceinte, you must know, which is why she has been spending so much time in bed. It took Mrs. Hennessey the same way. She felt dreadfully ill for the first three months, too. Though why she didn't tell the duke—Debora, I mean—except that he was so seldom home. And making her have all those horrid parties on top of the rest. It was really the outside of enough. Something had to be done, so we did it. She is going to cancel the pre-Christmas party and the Christmas party at Hastings, by the by. It is to be a condition of her remaining under Morland's roof."

"Shall we begin at the beginning?" he suggested, reining in his impatience.

"I thought I had. He was behaving badly, and we decided to show him a lesson. That's all. I was to meet him unchaperoned and let him kiss me. Debora was to catch us in flagrante delicto—or whatever it is called. I am not exactly sure what the phrase means. Then Debora was to announce she was leaving him, to scare him into behaving properly. And it worked. You saw them leave together."

Montaigne was not only mortified at his attack on Morland but miffed that he hadn't been allowed in on the plan. It sounded an excellent caper. He was also relieved and amused and felt a lingering desire to strike something or someone to relieve the pent-up aggravation.

"You might have let me know, and I wouldn't have come charging in, making a jackass of myself."

"You made a splendid jackass, Monty."

He glared. "Thank you. One does one's poor best."

"I think even Dick might have eventually figured out it was all put up if you hadn't come in at just that moment. That lent just the air of spontaneity the thing required. And he deserved that clout on the nose, too. But why *are* you here?"

"I hoped Meg would be home. I planned to visit with her until you arrived."

"Was there some particular reason you wished to see me?"

"Do I need an excuse?"

"No, I said a reason."

"Castlereagh is just back from Paris. I expect he was recalled to deal with this Holy Alliance business."

She frowned. "I am greatly interested to hear it. Thank you for rushing to me with that tidbit. I should hate to have to wait until the journals arrive to know of his return."

"Sarcasm ill becomes a young lady. What I was trying to say is that Margaret—Castlereagh's wife—is having a do this evening."

"Ah! And does she invite Whigs?"

"It is a purely social do. I am invited, along with a guest. I thought it might provide good research for you."

"I shall be happy to attend. Thank you, Monty." She waited, then said, "Was there anything else?"

A reluctant smile quirked his lips. He studied her a moment, his eyes brilliant with some constrained

181

emotion. "You have had enough seduction for one day. I shall call for you at nine."

"Actually you misconstrue the matter. I had to seduce the duke a little."

"I've created a monster! What am I going to do with you? If word of this gets about—"

"My reputation will be ruined!" she said, putting her hand to her brow in a melodramatic manner and swooning against the cushions. Then she looked up brightly. "But only think how it will sell books. There is nothing like a whiff of scandal. See what wonders it works for Byron."

"He's a man."

"Yes, it is much more dashing for a lady to be a flirt."

"You waste your talents writing pantomimes, miss. You ought to take to the boards. I shall call for you this evening." He bowed and left.

Cicely sat on alone, thinking.

Chapter Nineteen

Naturally Lady Fairly could not keep such a prime story as the duke's comeuppance to herself. She related it to half a dozen of her bosom bows that same evening over dinner. By the time Cicely and Montaigne arrived at the Castlereaghs' party, it was the evening's prime *on dit*. Eyebrows rose and nostrils pinched in disdain as she passed. There were enough of Montaigne's Whig friends present that Cicely was not sent to Coventry, but she certainly noticed her popularity had plummeted from its former height.

It was in the ladies' retirement parlor that she overheard two grand dames discussing her. She had gone behind a screen to adjust her stockings. Lady Spingle and Lady John Ashmore, née Alice and Susan McCurdle but still called jointly the McCurdle sisters, were famous gossips.

"I cannot imagine what Montaigne sees in her," one haughty voice complained. "A provincial nobody who fancies herself a bluestocking because she wrote one wretched novel. She was never even presented at Court. Let us hope Montaigne doesn't make the mistake of offering for her. She would be the ruination of his career."

"Oh my dear, you need not worry. Montaigne is too clever to make a mistake like that."

"Eldon says his work at the House has fallen off badly since she has come to Town. He is always in her pocket. It could well happen by accident—or design on her part. She arranged that unchaperoned tryst with Morland herself, you must know. No doubt that was an effort to get herself compromised and weasel an offer out of Montaigne. He feels responsible for her, as it seems he brought her to Town. A country neighbor. She stays with the Fairlys."

The ladies began walking toward the doorway. "And Lady Fairly is no better than she should be." The voices faded and vanished with the closing of the door.

Cicely stood on alone behind the screen, stunned. Is this what people, Montaigne's friends, thought of her? They were already cooler to him than before. Why had she been so selfish, taking Montaigne away from his work for practically a whole week, only to amuse her? She was destroying his reputation. She would return to Elmdale at once.

The revisions to her novel were done, the pantomime was in rehearsal, the party at Hastings had been canceled. There was nothing to keep her here, yet she hung on, waiting, hoping. Montaigne had invited her for a few days to attend Murray's dinner party, and she had turned it into an extended visit. Her head ached, and she suddenly felt nauseous. She summoned up her courage and went out in search of Montaigne.

She found him not far from the doorway, waiting for her.

"Hurry up, slowpoke!" he said. "The waltzes are just about to begin."

"I don't feel well, Montaigne. Would you mind taking me home?"

He could see at a glance that she was pale, with a drawn look about the eyes. He said at once, "Get your wrap. I'll make our excuses to Lady Castlereagh."

"What is the matter?" he asked as soon as they were in the carriage and on their way to Berkeley Square. "A tad too much wine?"

"I have a wretched headache," she said in a wan voice.

"I'll send for Dr. Knighton. Let us hope it is only a cold. A week in bed, and you'll be cured in time for the Christmas pantomime. Of course you won't be fit to travel for a while yet. This might get your papa to London."

His efforts to cheer her only cast her into deeper gloom.

"I would like to go home tomorrow, Montaigne. There is no reason for me to stay. I've done what I came here to do."

"Why, you have scarcely scratched the surface of what London has to offer. And you haven't bought your fur-lined cape yet. There are dozens of places we still have to visit."

"You are very kind, but I am imposing by staying so long, keeping you away from your work."

"There is no work for the next couple of weeks. The House is recessed."

"I am going home," she said firmly.

Montaigne began to suspect something had happened at the Castlereaghs'. The cats had been sharpening their claws in glee over the Morland

185

affair. "Did someone say something to you?" he asked. His voice held a sharp edge of annoyance, not at Cicely, but at whoever had spoken to her. "Some slur about that business with the Morlands? I know Meg was spreading the tale, the clunch. She paid a special call on Debora to get all the details. I shall ring a peal over her."

"It's not that."

"What is it, then? You were in high feather when we went to the party an hour ago. Now you are cast into gloom, ready to rush home to Elmdale. Something happened." He remembered seeing the McCurdle sisters coming out of the ladies' parlor just minutes before Cicely. "Did the McCurdle ladies say something to you?"

"Is that who they were?"

"I thought as much! What did they say?"

"They didn't say anything to me. I overheard them gossiping. You were right. I shouldn't have stuck my nose into the Morlands' business. But it is no matter. It is time to go home in any case. Any little scandal will only be a nine days' wonder. It won't reflect on you, once I'm out of your hair."

"So that's what they said. That you are ruining my career, the ninnyhammers."

He laughed and tried to talk away her fears. No one paid any heed to the McCurdles. The incident would be forgotten in a day or two. London was a hotbed of gossip. But Cicely was determined. When they reached Berkeley Square she was still insisting that she would leave the next day.

Montaigne accompanied her into the house. "Why don't you return to the party? It is still early," she pointed out.

"I have something I want to say to you."

186

The butler took their things and they went into the saloon, where a fire burned in the grate. It was welcome after the cold winds of December. The room was warm, but it didn't remove the chill from Cicely's heart. She gave Montaigne an accusing look. A moment's consideration told her that the quickest way to get rid of him was to hear him out. She felt he was only going to try to talk her into staying longer and was prepared to resist his urgings to the last gasp.

Montaigne seemed nervous. He poured two glasses of wine, handed her one, and emptied his own glass in one shot. Then he put the glass down, straightened his shoulders, cleared his throat, and began.

"I hadn't meant to speak until I had an opportunity to discuss it with Mr. Caldwell first. Sissie, I want to marry you."

"Oh no!" she howled. His businesslike pronouncement sounded strained. Nothing in either his face or his voice suggested love. It was the voice of duty, just what those two ladies had prophesied. He felt responsible for the mess she had made of her reputation. Being a gentleman, he was ready to pay the price.

His first expression of shock at her outburst soon turned to uncertainty. "It cannot come as a complete surprise to you after the events of the past weeks?" he said questioningly.

"How dare you! Are you implying I schemed to force you into it?"

"Certainly not! That was not my meaning. I think we would deal very well together."

"No, you do not think anything of the sort. And you don't fool me, either. You think I have compromised

187

myself, and it will end up in your dish, since you brought me to London."

"I love you, damn it!"

"It sounds like it!" she shot back. "If you could see the scowl on your face! Oh, I wish I had never come to London. I wish I had never heard of Debora, with her purple eyes, and Morland, with his horrid dinner parties and diamonds. I am going home tomorrow, Montaigne."

"That's impossible. I can't get away tomorrow," he said.

"We are not quite Siamese twins. I don't expect you to come with me. If you would just lend me your traveling coach—"

"The wheels need mending," he invented.

"Then I shall take the public coach."

"That you will not. I brought you here, and I shall take you home. We can leave in the afternoon. My carriage should be repaired by then."

"Very well."

"But I wish you would reconsider. I am serious about wanting to marry you, Cicely."

She glared. "Don't patronize me, Montaigne. You might spare me that at least." She set down her glass and strode from the room, because if she stayed one more minute, she knew the tears would spurt.

As soon as Montaigne was alone, he unleashed a litany of accomplished curses. As this did not even begin to soothe his wrath, he threw the glass into the grate, where it shattered with a very satisfying crash. He strode into the hallway, snatched up his hat and cape before the butler could reach them, and let himself out into the cold wind.

He drove straight to his own mansion on

Grosvenor Square. He knew he had made a botch of his proposal. He also knew that Cicely was too proud to accept an offer tinged with obligation on his part. He would have to prove to her satisfaction that he truly loved her. She had called him a romantic lunatic. Very well, then, he would live up to his reputation and contrive a romantically lunatic method to prove it.

What weighed on his mind as he made his tentative plans was whether she loved him. A genuine refusal was a possibility, and must be taken into account. With luck, he should have a reply from her papa in the morning mail, and the completely outrageous plan that was hatching in his devious mind would not have to be executed. But if Caldwell refused Montaigne's invitation to London to attend the Christmas pantomime . . .

He rooted through desk and cupboards in search of a map of England and his copy of the *Traveler's Guide*. These were not necessary for a trip to Elmdale. He knew that route like the back of his hand. It was the Great North Road that he studied with considerable interest. He marked an X on the map at Chesham, where his cousin Thorold lived. If Montaigne delayed their departure long enough, they would not get farther than twenty-odd miles tomorrow.

While Montaigne laid his scheme for her abduction, Cicely asked the servants to bring her trunk down from the attic and began sorting out her packing. Other than her under linens and outer garments, she might as well not have unpacked, she had worn so few of her own outfits. She regretfully left Meg's dashing gowns hanging in the closet. Each dress brought a memory—and a fresh pang to

189

her heart. There was the green one she had worn to Murray's dinner, when she brought Sir Giles around her finger. Here the rose one she had worn to the theater. The ivory and chicken-skin fan and the peacock fan, retrieved from Morland's grate and not so very burned, went in along with the rest, a reminder of her folly. Anne's blue stockings were placed in Cook's graduated beaker and added to the trunk.

She would have liked to get to know Debora better. There was more to her than her violet eyes. Cicely suspected it was her being enceinte and Dick's lack of concern that made Debora appear apathetic. She had entered into conning the duke with excellent spirits. After her confinement, she might have proved a good friend. Naturally Montaigne would not have fallen in love with a lady who had only a beautiful face to attract him.

It was fatally easy to distract her thoughts to Montaigne. He couldn't possibly love her. He was offering only out of a sense of duty. How stiffly he had spoken, how reluctantly. "I want to marry you," he had said. Just cropped out bluntly with the necessary words, no lovemaking. He hadn't even told her he loved her, except in that horrid, angry way. *"I love you, damn it!"* What sort of a proposal was that? It was not the way Ravencroft had proposed to Eugenie.

Cicely had seen too much of arranged marriages to consign herself to such a fate. And if a lady were so foolish as to actually love a husband who did not love her, the situation would be completely intolerable. Indifferences would soon sink to despisement. Much better to go home to Elmdale and try to find some small measure of peace by writing it all up disguised as fiction.

She had come to London to find out about life, and she had found out—more than she bargained for.

Chapter Twenty

The morning post brought Montaigne no reply from his invitation to the Caldwells. The abduction was on. He paid a call on the archbishop of Canterbury and procured a special license to marry without the banns being called in church.

On Berkeley Square, Cicely argued the morning away with Meg and Fairly, who took it as a personal affront that she should leave them just when she had become such an object of curiosity among the ton. Now that Fairly had his arm out of a sling, they were after a new novelty to astound Society.

Cicely hoped that Montaigne's vague "afternoon" meant literally after twelve noon. By one o'clock she knew this was not the case. By two, she was becoming extremely frustrated at the delay but sat down to lunch with Meg, as Montaigne was obviously lunching elsewhere and Cicely didn't want to leave with an empty stomach. Immediately after lunch, Fairly left for his club. A few flakes of snow had begun to drift down. Not enough to make travel impossible, although the leaden sky showed no sign of fair weather in the immediate future.

At three o'clock, Montaigne's traveling carriage and team of four finally arrived.

"Sorry I'm late. I got held up, but we still have a few hours of daylight."

Cicely noticed that he was in remarkably good spirits for a gentleman who pretended he didn't want her to leave. It would be dark within the hour at this time of year. He was delighted to be rid of her, and who should blame him?

"We'd best be off if we hope to make it home before the storm breaks," she said peevishly.

Meg's sniffs of annoyance gave way to tears and promises to write. Hugs were exchanged and at last the carriage was off.

Montaigne took the precaution of leaving London by the same route as they had arrived, to prevent Cicely from becoming suspicious. She looked forlornly out the window as the glories of the West End dwindled to the mediocrity of the outskirts of town. She didn't notice when the carriage veered north. To avoid conversation, she had claimed fatigue and sat with her eyes closed, pretending to be asleep. Montaigne let her rest, happy that she was unaware of the direction they were taking.

About an hour later, when they stopped at a tollgate, Cicely became tired of feigning sleep and opened her eyes.

"I don't remember this tollgate," she said, peering out the window.

"They all look much alike. The snow is coming down a little faster now," he added, to distract her.

A glance at the window showed her the few flakes had turned into a regular snowfall. A spasm of alarm seized her. "What if we have to stop before we get home? Overnight, I mean, at an inn or something."

"Then you'll just have to marry me," he said, and laughed.

"It's not funny, Montaigne!" she scowled. "That is exactly what those McCurdle ladies meant. I shan't marry you, I don't care if we have to spend the whole winter alone in some abandoned house."

"You would rather destroy my reputation?" he asked, still joking, but with a tinge of concern.

"Perhaps we should turn back," she said doubtfully. "We haven't gone far."

"John Groom will get us through," Montaigne said firmly.

His reply convinced Cicely he was happy to be getting her out of town, out of his hair.

The falling snow made it difficult to see much of the surroundings as the carriage continued on its way north. Before long, the sun had set, to complete the oblivion beyond the carriage. When they came to an intersection, the coachman stopped the carriage and got out to read the signpost. Curious to see how far they had come, Cicely said, "I'm going to get out."

"Better not. You're only wearing slippers."

"The snow hasn't piled up yet."

She opened the door herself and hopped out. Montaigne followed her, preparing excuses in case the signpost gave him away, as indeed it did.

The wind snatched at Cicely's pelisse and flung it about. Snowflakes whirled through the air, catching in her hair. Where the light from the coachman's lamp caught them, they sparkled and flashed. Drifted snow gathered against hedges and in ruts in the road, causing splotches of white in the surrounding darkness. She peered at the signpost.

"That sign says St. Albans, Ten Miles," she exclaimed. "We're going the wrong way, Montaigne. We are heading north."

"Right ahead is our turn off to the west," he explained. He winked at John Groom over Cicely's head. "You know the shortcut, Harelson."

"Have no fear, lordship. I'll get you where you want to go."

The carriage did soon make a turn. Disoriented in a strange place, Cicely assumed they were heading west. Another turn soon brought them back northward. They continued for another hour. The snow came in fits and starts, sometimes forming a moving lace curtain in the darkness beyond the carriage window, sometimes disappearing. They reached Chesham during a lull in the snowfall. The sign proclaiming Chesham was large enough to be legible from the carriage. Cicely had to lower the window to read the smaller print below, giving directions to the Great North Road.

She turned and stared at Montaigne, who was also reading the sign. His expression showed not the least concern, but a definite touch of satisfaction.

"Montaigne! Is it possible you are kidnapping me?" she asked in a choked voice. She lowered her head to her raised hands and erupted into a strangled burst of laughter.

As laughter was the last thing Montaigne expected to hear, he easily mistook her response for tears. "Cicely, I can explain!"

"No, no!" she said, shaking with the effort to conceal her soaring joy.

Montaigne moved to the banquette beside her and drew her into his arms. "How else could I convince you I want to marry you?" he asked.

195

"Gretna Green?" she asked in a strangled whisper.

"If you hate the idea, we can turn back and be in London before midnight. No one need know. I didn't tell Meg. Don't cry, my dear. It was a foolish thing for me to do."

His arms held her warm and close in the darkness of the carriage. When she didn't draw away, he removed her bonnet and stroked her hair with loving fingers, while soft words of endearment were showered on her.

"I think I have loved you from the moment you roundly condemned *Chaos*. Or perhaps it was when you flirted that old slice, Gresham, into pretending he didn't despise it. You would be happy in London, darling. I could make you happy."

Cicely made no reply, but only snuggled her head into the crook of his neck, trying to assimilate that this was really happening, that Montaigne loved her. He tilted her face up to see what expression she wore and saw the laughter there. When she drew her lower lip between her teeth to stifle the merriment, he felt as if he had been kicked in the stomach by a mule. She wasn't even angry, only laughing at his clownish attempt at romance.

"I see you are amused at my folly," he said, stiff with embarrassment. "I'll tell John Groom to take us to Berkeley Square."

"Oh, Monty! How divinely romantic! I could never understand how you wrote *Chaos*, but I see now you really are perfectly romantic and ridiculous beneath your businesslike facade. Kidnapping, Gretna Green, and a wedding over the anvil! It is worthy of Ravencroft. You must really love me if—"

His lips seized hers in a passionate kiss, bringing

her outpourings to a stop. His strong hands were gentle as they stroked her cheeks and caressed the nape of her neck. They brushed warmly down her throat, as if he had to touch her to confirm that she was there, and happy.

His gentleness made her feel loved and wanted without feeling threatened by his passion. When she responded warmly to Montaigne's touch, his arms went around her to crush the breath out of her. Cicely shyly looped her arms around his neck and returned the pressure. It seemed strangely intimate to feel his crisp hair between her fingers. A quivering excitement stirred Cicely to the innermost core of her being. As the kiss deepened, she felt a melting warmth invade her. It grew to an aching, primitive longing as the excitement swelled to consume her in its flames.

Later, when Montaigne loosened his grip and gazed down into Cicely's upturned face, he saw she wore an expression of perfect enchantment. It was a look as old as time, yet as new and thrilling as their love. A look that would be etched into his memory for all time.

His voice was rough with emotion when he said, "Of course I love you, you sweet idiot. Didn't I tell you so last night?"

"Naturally you had to pretend you did after those horrid ladies said those things."

"I didn't have to pretend," he said firmly and kissed her again for her folly.

"And you don't have to ruin your career by a runaway match, either—though it was a lovely idea," she said, and drew a deep, blissful sigh.

"We could still do it! Let's!"

"No, let us enjoy the anticipation a little longer. And Papa, you know—"

"Yes, you're right, of course."

As the carriage began to move, Montaigne opened the window and called, "Back to town, Harelson. We've changed our minds."

"As you like, your lordship."

He closed the window and turned back to Cicely. "Now where were we?" he asked in a softly intimate voice and drew her into his arms to continue his lovemaking.

The return journey seemed to pass much more quickly than the trip north. The roads were becoming clogged with snow by the time they reached Berkeley Square. The Fairlys were out, but the lights were still burning belowstairs. Coddle admitted them. He didn't make any inquiries, but his raised eyebrow suggested curiosity.

"I was taking Miss Cicely home, but we decided we couldn't make it in this storm, so I brought her back here," Montaigne said.

"Very wise decision, if I may say so, milord."

"The Fairlys are out?"

Coddle nodded. "I expect they will return early, as the snow is worsening. Would you care for tea, Miss Cicely, and perhaps a snack?"

"That would be lovely, thank you, Coddle."

They went into the saloon. Montaigne applied the poker to the banked coals in the grate. A shower of sparks flew up, and soon a good fire was burning. There was much to discuss before he left. He confessed that he had written to Mr. Caldwell asking him for permission to marry Cicely and inviting him to London for the pantomime.

"Why didn't you tell me, Monty?"

"Because I'm a romantic lunatic. I wanted everything to be perfect, with your papa and Anne here."

"Everything *is* perfect," she said, squeezing his fingers. "Now Papa will come. My little play would not budge him, but marriage to Lord Montaigne! That is a more admirable achievement." She gave him an arch smile and added, "In Papa's eyes, I mean."

"Wretch!" The word was a caress.

Wild horses would not have kept Mr. Caldwell away when he read the charmed words, "I wish to apply for permission to marry your younger daughter. You are aware of my worldly circumstances, I think." The letter continued for another page, with details of the visit to London.

It would be hard to tell whether Anne or Mr. Caldwell was happier at the news. Mr. Caldwell's letter of permission was dispatched posthaste and arrived with Montaigne's post the morning after the aborted flight to Gretna Green. Caldwell and Anne left the next day for London. Once Cicely's family was at Grosvenor Square, she was permitted to join them at Montaigne's palatial mansion. She was extremely gratified at her fiancé's treatment of them, which was thoughtful and generous without showing the least touch of condescension.

They spent a week being shown around town by Montaigne and Cicely. Their guests made an excellent excuse to return to *King Lear* and actually watch the play.

It was arranged that the wedding would take place at home in the middle of January.

"I must acquire my trousseau," Cicely pointed out

when Montaigne wished to make use of the special license.

"The banns take three weeks!" he cried, as if it were three years.

"Papa already arranged that with the vicar before he left Elmdale. There is no getting out of it, milord."

"I'm happy you are aware of it, miss."

Lord Montaigne made his fiancée a betrothal gift of a sable-lined cape. With her check for *Georgiana* in her pocket, Cicely bought a slightly less grand fur-lined garment for Anne. The ladies looked as fine as ninepence as they sat in a box on the grand tier for the premier performance of Cicely's Christmas pantomime. Mr. Caldwell could not have been happier if Cicely were marrying a royal prince.

The Fairlys filled the other two seats. The Duke and Duchess of Morland had retired to Hastings, so Anne was not able to see the living model of Eugenie, about whom she had heard so much. She not only saw Mr. Witherspoon but found him so attractive that she encouraged Montaigne to include him in several of their outings. Society could not be hard on Miss Cicely when her brazen behavior had yielded the excellent result of catching herself a lord. The McCurdle ladies were two voices crying in the wilderness.

The short pantomime was received with great applause. The audience laughed in all the right places and clapped loudly at its termination. But the greatest thrill for Cicely was to see, on the playbill and program, CHRISTMAS SKETCH BY MISS CICELY CALDWELL. The program was carefully placed away with her souvenirs.

To return his generosity, Caldwell invited Montaigne to spend Christmas at Elmdale. They arrived on the evening of the twenty-fourth. The house was redolent with the aroma of fir boughs that decorated the doorways and hung in swags along the banister and mantel. A crackling fire in the grate lent a welcome warmth and light to that grand chamber. Cook had prepared a pot of mulled wine that hung on the fireplace hook to welcome them.

Anne hastened off to speak to Cook as soon as she had taken off her bonnet and fur-lined pelisse. Mr. Caldwell sent for his steward to learn how the estate had managed without him during his absence. Cicely was left alone with Montaigne in the saloon. She walked to the window to gaze out at the wintry scene before her. The boughs of the soaring spruce in front of the window were heavy with snow, but the night was clear. Pinpricks of numberless stars twinkled in the black velvet sky.

Montaigne went to look over Cicely's shoulder. He slipped his arm around her waist and pulled her against him.

"A beautiful night," he murmured. "I always find myself looking for the star of Bethlehem on Christmas Eve."

"I pretend the North Star is it," she replied, peering up in search of it.

Then she turned around. "Do you know, Monty, it was just one month ago that you came here and asked me to let on I had written *Chaos Is Come Again*. What a month! I have been to London and met all sorts of interesting people, I have sold my novel, and had my little sketch performed. Why, if I ever put that into a book, everyone would say it was a fairy tale. And on top of it all— Why are you looking like that?" she asked as he frowned playfully at her.

"What you have outlined is merely a success story. Your first-class fairy tale would provide a Prince Charming and a wedding."

A slow smile formed, lifting Cicely's lips and softening her eyes with love. "I was going to say that! I was saving the best for the last."

"Am I the best? Who said caparisons are odious?"

"Mrs. Malaprop, wasn't it?" When he shook his head in frustration, she added, "Eugenie would have given a better answer, but I am not Eugenie."

"No, you are not, and I thank God for it," Montaigne said, drawing her into his arms.

Over his shoulder, Cicely spotted the North Star. "There! There is the Christmas star!" she cried.

Montaigne just glanced at it. His Christmas star was here, in his arms.